The Rome Apartment

BOOKS BY KERRY FISHER

The Rome Apartment

Kerry Fisher

bookouture

Published by Bookouture in 2023

An imprint of Storyfire Ltd.
Carmelite House
50 Victoria Embankment
London EC4Y oDZ

www.bookouture.com

ISBN: 978-1-83790-048-0
eBook ISBN: 978-1-83790-047-3

To the wonderful women I met travelling in my twenties, who are still part of my journey today.

PROLOGUE

RONNIE

A birthday card posted to arrive on time from England to Italy was a sign of commitment. Organisation, for sure. But not necessarily love. Just seeing my daughter's handwriting on the envelope – central, tidy, *dutiful* – stirred that familiar feeling in me, that I'd failed her, that my desire to leave the past behind had stopped me investing fully in the future, in case life turned on a sixpence again.

I ripped open the envelope. At the age of seventy-four, I really needed to get over the disappointment of the single bald line of italic type – Happy Birthday – on the card. I could never admit that I lusted after one of those fancy varieties with lots of inserts, detailing exactly how I'd been a wonderful mother.

I unfolded the letter inside. I imagined Nadia slipping her posh pen out of its case, calling, 'What shall I write to Mum?' across the kitchen, while Grant won husband of the year cooking up some show-offy dinner, all miso paste and truffle dust, served up in such a tiny portion that I'd be dreaming of a great big ciabatta stuffed with prosciutto and cheese the second I got up from the table.

I scanned the first few lines and my heart dropped.

Now Zia Laura has moved to Bologna to be with Cousin Simone, I was wondering if it would be okay for Grant and me to come and live in her apartment next door for a few months in the spring? We can both work from home, though we'd probably have to nip over to England now and again for the occasional meeting. It would be good to stay in Rome for a long-ish spell – I'd really like Grant to get to know the city properly rather than the flying visits he's used to.

She went on to say that she worried about me living by myself since her dad died and Laura had moved away, and what a good opportunity it would be for us to spend some time together when we weren't planning a funeral and sorting out Matteo's stuff.

The truth was, though, we got on better at a distance. After a couple of days, our 'so lovely to see you' veneer would wear off. Nadia would start nagging me. About how it made sense for me to move back to England to be closer to her. She had no idea why I left for Italy in the first place, the emotional cost every time I gathered myself to return to Britain. I couldn't face an extended period of her badgering me. And that was before she got onto the minor things: my diet, how much parmesan I sprinkled over my pasta – 'Mum, it's so salty. It's not good for your blood pressure'; when exactly I was going to give up riding my Vespa, hovering like the Grim Reaper with her 'If you have an accident at your age...'

Nope. The last thing I needed was Nadia and her husband establishing themselves next door and monitoring my every move, with an opinion about what I ate, what I wore, where I went... 'You shouldn't be hanging around for the bus late at night, Mum.' Ha. She was right. I didn't take the bus late at night. Instead, I whipped along on my Vespa in all weathers, always choosing the Lungotevere – the roads that adjoined the river – where I could. I would never tire of those glorious bridges and the street lamps reflecting into the water. After more than forty years in Rome, the sight of the lights sparkling across the surface of the river still held that sense of mystery, of ancient charm and romantic promise that had kept me here in the first place.

I couldn't have Nadia here for months. While we lived in different countries, she could fit me into her life, shoehorn me into twenty minutes of FaceTime on a Monday night before Grant got home from badminton. I could reassure myself in those short, sharp bursts that although her life, dominated as it was by restriction and rules, wasn't my idea of fun, she was happy.

But therein lay the problem. Nadia fell into the trap of thinking that there was only one way to be happy – her way. Choosing not to have children because the world was overpopulated. Railing against people who wasted water by leaving the tap running when they were cleaning their teeth. Lecturing me on what I was eating when we spoke – avocados contributing to the demise of the rainforest, as well as chocolate – 'Have you any idea how much wildlife habitat has been destroyed by the big confectionery companies?' Haranguing me about how to eat as though I'd entered my eighth decade without having a clue – 'Don't shovel it in, Mum. You need to chew mindfully. Savour the flavours. It helps keep your weight down.'

I admired her principles. I really did. However, I still didn't want her applying her high standards to my life. Women my age – *any* age – weren't supposed to look like cocktail sticks. In fact, the only standards I was really interested in at this stage of my life were my own. Which were to live without rationing joy or navigating the time I had left on earth between two crispbreads washed down with spring water filtered through limestone rocks.

I'd had nearly forty years of Matteo having a view about when it was acceptable to have a drink with ice without it causing abdominal cramps, or complaining about *mal di fegato* – liver ache – which I was pretty sure no English person had ever suffered from. Not to mention his penchant for suppositories. What sane person stuck paracetamol up their backside to bring down a fever? One of the few things I loved about my farming parents was their attitude to illness: 'If you're still sucking in air, get on with it.'

I could say quite honestly – though I'd have to pick my audience wisely if I was going to voice it out loud – that three out of the five years since my husband died were the most liberating I'd ever experienced. Two years to readjust everything I'd assumed I knew and three to rejoice in the business of living without caring what anyone thought. If only I'd realised how refreshing that was, I wouldn't have waited so long to get cracking.

Since Nadia had disappeared off to England soon after Matteo died, she'd only caught fleeting glimpses of the unfettered me. Even I could rein it in for our weekly call and with a bit of preparation I could just about survive when they visited for a long weekend. Last Easter, though, when Grant was pontificating about the importance of having my cholesterol tested, I did have to take to my bed with a pretend headache and a secret stash of Baci chocolates. Oh, the rebellion of gobbling up the melting loveliness and letting my mind ponder the possibilities of the little paper message wrapped around each one: 'My love, kiss me now in these meadows full of birdsong.'

Nadia was probably talking about 'my elderly mother in Italy', when, on a good day, I felt younger at seventy-four than I had at fifty-four. Whatever life I had left, I was going to ride out in embracing the unexpected, learning new things, finding people and situations to challenge my thinking, disregarding the limitations that my daughter thought age should bestow upon me. I was going to live unfiltered.

And that meant making sure she and Grant didn't take up residence where they could do a daily inventory of my behaviour.

I pressed my fingers to my eyes. My Italian friends would be scandalised by the fact that I wanted to pass up the prospect of having my daughter installed next door, where we could share every moment of each other's lives. But I knew myself, and I knew Nadia. A little bit of distance was a balm, not a hindrance, to our relationship.

A knock at the door saved my brain from running around to discover something that looked like a compromise. I flung the door open to find my upstairs neighbour, Marina, standing there with a cake. I eyed the thick icing, my memory darting to the carrot and beetroot cake Nadia had horrified my friends with last year.

'*Auguri!*' Marina came in and marched through to my kitchen with the determined stride of someone who didn't need to stand on ceremony given what she knew about my life. You couldn't keep anything a secret when you lived in an apartment, even one with thick walls contained within a grand old Italian house. 'Never too old for cake.'

I obviously failed to muster up my usual cheer at the sight of Marina's baking. She observed me suspiciously.

'What? What's happened?'

Her eyes dropped to the card and letter on the table.

'Oh that's grand. Nadia remembered your birthday.'

It still made me smile when Marina said, 'That's grand' in pure Dublinese learnt from her Irish dad with a slight Italian inflection. Nadia had the same fluent English but with an unusual cadence that would pique the curiosity of a native speaker.

'Actually, it's not grand.'

I explained what Nadia was planning.

'The thing is, I can't say outright, "I don't want you here, you mustn't come."' I hesitated. 'It would be lovely to spend some time with her, but both of them together, well, you know.'

Marina nodded. 'They could stay in my beach house at Santa Marinella. She could still pop up here by train. We'd have to get cleaners in, though. I haven't been since before the pandemic.'

'That's very generous of you, *cara*. I might have to take you up on that. She wouldn't want to live in either of the two apartments I was planning to do up and rent out before COVID until I've sorted out the kitchen and bathrooms anyway. But it doesn't solve why she can't move into Laura's old place.' My voice trailed away.

Marina had been touchy about my plan to let out another part of the building, because after being a tenant in the palazzo's third-floor apartment for over twenty years, she deemed herself to have a say in the matter – 'What if the people turn out to be horrible? Then you're stuck with them for four years.' I preferred to think that the Italian rental system gave everyone stability, but Marina's commitment to social justice wavered if it showed any signs of inconveniencing her.

'I think more clearly when I've had some sugar,' Marina said, fetching a knife from the drawer and cutting the cake. 'I didn't think you'd want seventy-four candles.'

I laughed. 'Too right. But I'm not going to complain about getting older. A privilege denied to many and all that.'

I put the espresso maker on the gas and heated up some milk. Marina was used to me drinking milky coffee way after any Italian deemed it acceptable. Enduring decades of 'Cappuccino at this hour?' hadn't ever converted me to drinking a tiny espresso. I couldn't see the point of them.

Marina settled into the squidgy corner sofa I'd bought to replace the heavy brown furniture we'd inherited from Matteo's parents. 'Why don't you tell her that you've found tenants for

Laura's apartment?' she asked, brushing the crumbs from her mouth.

'You know what she's like, Marina. She'll want to know details, who, what, where. I can't lie to her.'

'So let it out for real.'

Somehow, the energy I'd had for maximising my income by renovating and renting out the other two apartments pre-COVID had given way to an appreciation of the simple life and the peace that reigned in our building. I sagged at the thought of rental agents, cleaners, finding the right furniture, interviewing prospective residents, fixing or explaining the many quirks woven into the DNA of an ancient palazzo. And yes, Marina and her multiple opinions.

'I'm too old to be living next door to families clattering in and out at all hours. And I rather like my women-only apartment block. It's quite nice not to have any men telling us what to do,' I said, while recognising the irony that the only reason I lived here in the first place was because I'd inherited it from my husband.

Marina laughed. 'I am the ideal tenant. If you advertised for British women, they'd have to leave after three months anyway because of the Brexit restrictions. Even better if they're older than say, forty, so we don't have to put up with the shenanigans of youth.'

I ignored Marina's delusions about her own perfection. 'But how would I go about finding middle-aged British women? And I think three months is too long. Maybe two and a half with a possibility of extending to three if it all goes well?'

'There must be somewhere you can advertise that would attract that sort of person.'

'*The Lady*? I'm sure that has a lot of adverts for different arrangements abroad. That's where I found my housekeeping job here all those years ago.'

There was a silence as we both considered how that one decision had shaped the rest of my life.

I pressed on. 'We need to attract the right type of person. A woman who's going to make the most of Rome. We don't want someone hanging around the garden with a long face or whining about the church bells waking them up or nit-picking about the Italians. I mean, we can do that, but we don't want to import criticism.'

Marina stood up to cut herself another large slice of cake. There was a reason we got on well. She sat down again, pushing the plate towards me. 'Here, feed that big brain of yours. How do we entice a single middle-aged woman from England to Rome?'

'Promise them romance?'

Marina snorted. 'We'd get had up under Trades Descriptions. With all our disastrous marriages between us, I think we've used up our romance-finding quotient. You're the one who moved to Italy and stayed here. What kept you here? What stopped you going back to the UK after all that business with Matteo?'

Marina had always been able to do that. Pinpoint the crux of the matter.

'Rome has such energy, such beauty. When I first came here, I used to get up at six o'clock every morning to enjoy the empty streets before I went to work. I walked miles, peering through doorways, looking up at the stone masonry, heading up into the hills to see the sunrise over the city. I felt so alive. As though I'd barely been existing up until then. It was also so liberating to escape everyone who knew me, everyone who had a view on who I was.' I didn't take the sentence to its logical conclusion, allowing 'And what I'd done' to remain tucked away in my own head.

Even Marina didn't know the whole story. And I wasn't going to blight my birthday by thinking about it.

Marina suddenly sat bolt upright on the sofa, her large bosom jiggling with enthusiasm. 'I've got it! Why don't you advertise for a middle-aged woman who's lost her va-va-voom?'

I frowned. 'That sounds like an advert for an energy drink. Or soliciting for sex.'

Marina shook her head. 'No, I mean, a woman of a certain age who's lost her sparkle. Maybe because of a cheating rotten scoundrel.' Marina's English sometimes took on a 1940s film-star quality when she was excited. 'Or maybe her kids have left home and she's not sure who she is any more. We can help her reconnect with her *raison d'être*.'

I wrinkled my nose. 'I'm not sure I want to be responsible for nurse-maiding a stranger through their mid-life crisis.'

'Come on. What could be more satisfying than seeing some worn-out woman blossom? And anyhow, we don't have to do it ourselves. We only have to point her in the right direction. The sunshine and the beauty of the city will do the rest. Like it did for you all those years ago. Sometimes you need a bit of space to rediscover who you are when no one is categorising you. We can draw up a list of things they have to do while they're here to help them on their way.'

Forget the candles. And at a push, the cake too. In her own inimitable style, Marina appeared to have delivered the ultimate gift. Planning how to keep my own freedom and grant someone else theirs was all the birthday celebration I needed.

1

_____

BETH

Not for the first time, I marvelled at the universe's ability to balance out one person's gain with another person's loss – my daughter, Maddie, getting to Leeds University versus my pain at waving goodbye to my only child, knowing that the next time I saw her she'd have shifted away from me towards all the possibilities that glittered out there in the world. It was right and just and a cause for celebration. But as I looked around her campus room with its brand new duvet and the fish oil and multivitamins I'd optimistically lined up on the windowsill, I felt only loss. Bereft of the purpose that had driven me for eighteen years, alongside a heartache so physical that I could see Meryl Streep singing 'Slipping Through My Fingers' in my mind's eye.

Maddie was peering over my shoulder, into the corridor, twitching to cast off her parents and burst into the exciting melee of new people beyond. I hoped there'd be another lovely girl in her hall of residence, someone who'd make sure she went to the doctor's if her tonsilitis flared up again, who'd want to share buying groceries and who knew how to cook more than pasta. I hovered, straightening her pillows, knowing I had to go, yet feeling that I hadn't uttered the right words, the ones that would make her think, keep her safe without me.

Joel made the break. He stepped forward, handing her sixty pounds and saying, 'That's emergency money for a taxi. Don't walk back from anywhere on your own late at night.'

They hugged while I thought my chest would burst from the effort of not crying.

Joel nodded towards the door. 'Come on, Beth, say your goodbyes and we'll leave her to it.'

I wanted to run out into the hallway and grab one of the other kids and facilitate the introductions so she wouldn't be sitting here on her own. I pulled her to me. 'As soon as we've gone, you should go into the kitchen and get to know the others.'

'Mum. I'll be fine.'

That undid me. Recognising that the little girl, who had to be peeled off me when she started reception, didn't need me. In fact, she looked for all the world as though she couldn't wait to shake off who she was and where she'd come from. She was poised to experiment with new opinions and identities to create an entirely different human. One that would no doubt have views, clothing and drinking habits way beyond anything her stuffy old parents might deem acceptable.

I blundered out of her room in an unseemly muddle, past a boy carrying his gym weights, and out into the fresh air. I turned the knife on myself by staring up at her window with the curtains that hung crookedly to see if she was waving. She wasn't.

Tears poured out of me. I wanted Joel to take my hand and tell me that this would pass, that I wouldn't feel so hollow and redundant by tomorrow morning. I wanted him to tease me gently, make me giggle about getting in a state over something that was a good thing, a positive springboard for Maddie rather than the funereal event I appeared to be turning it into. But he'd retreated into himself, as he often did in times of extreme emotion. Maybe he was floundering about for his own brave face and didn't want to admit it.

He walked several steps ahead, with the briefest glance behind to see if I was following. I hurried after him, my mind whirling with all the things I forgot to say, to warn Maddie about.

My eyes snagged on another couple, the mother swiping at her face, shaking her head and saying over and over, 'I don't know why I'm so upset'.

Her husband smiled and said, 'Because we'll miss him.' He threw his arm around her shoulder. 'Hopefully, it's not because you're stuck with me on your own.' She laughed through her tears. 'I'm actually looking forward to having your full atten-tion,' he said, leaning in to kiss her on her forehead.

As I hurried after Joel as he disappeared into the car park, I couldn't help but feel envious. I wanted Joel to acknowledge that, for me, this was a hard stage of motherhood, the end of my day-to-day role of parenting, of being the first touchstone for Maddie, of sharing her world by osmosis rather than by permission.

I reached the car, where Joel was programming the satnav to take us home. He looked up as I got in. 'You can have a life without Maddie, you know, a kind of new start for you.' His tone was gentle, but also seemed to hold a rebuke, as though whatever I'd been doing to date had been self-indulgent and pointless and I finally had the opportunity to make something of myself.

I wasn't the sort to bite back. I liked everything smooth and harmonious, ordered. But I'd just witnessed first-hand how some husbands could look past themselves and empathise with their wives, even if they weren't experiencing the separation from their child with the same intensity. 'Sorry, but I'm not being dramatic on purpose. My rational self knows that this is a wonderful thing for Maddie. It will just take some adjusting. I know it's not logical, but feelings often aren't.'

Joel leaned back against the headrest. 'I do understand. Really I do. But everything has been about Maddie for the last eighteen years, about keeping the house ticking over and everything stable so she can have the best start. And now she has, so it's our turn. It will really do you good to branch out a bit more, take advantage of different opportunities.'

I felt the burn of injustice. I *had* given priority to Maddie, and I'd also turned down a couple of promotions when she was younger, but I'd still worked as a full-time tax specialist for the last ten years and overseen a whole team of accountants. Joel was making it sound as though I hadn't progressed from my first graduate job. In fact, one of the reasons I loved my work was that I knew I was good at it, the only arena where I wasn't always second-guessing myself. Everyone always talked about me as a safe pair of hands, calm in a crisis. The most difficult customers and cases were often passed to me – 'Beth's steady under fire.' I'd taken pride in being the person everyone counted on. Yet Joel was talking about me as if I'd been stabbing away at the same few buttons on a calculator for the last two decades.

In a quiet voice, I said, 'I don't regret any of the decisions I've made. I've still managed to become pretty senior at work and I think Maddie's had a happy childhood.' I resisted the temptation to point out the inconvenient fact that Joel's patchy work history meant there wasn't much room for me to take risks that might jeopardise my job security.

Joel sighed. 'But there's more to life than clocking in on time and making sure everyone's had their broccoli provision for the week.'

I wasn't quite sure why Joel had chosen now to have a go at me. Especially as it was easy to make statements like that when he had the luxury of me accomplishing all the boring but necessary functions. My diligence had allowed him to hang onto his lofty ideas about only taking on corporate accounting projects that sounded 'challenging and fulfilling' rather than focusing on keeping a roof over our heads and dinner on the table.

I turned towards him, waiting for him to suggest an adventure that would take me right out of my comfort zone, sailing around the Caribbean islands or some hideous jungle trek that he'd been talking about doing 'when it's just the two of us'. I was preparing to shake my head, that the timing was wrong, that I couldn't think about holidays right now.

But he didn't say anything. He fell silent. Not a lumpy, ill-tempered silence, the sort that twenty-four years of marriage delivers when one spouse is a bit out of sorts and momentarily broods about how perfect their existence could be were it not for their partner's shortcomings. No, this was a loaded quiet, laden with suppressed fury.

In normal circumstances, I'd dance around it, defaulting to promises to make Joel's favourite food and offering to take on researching builders to turn our garage into a home office for him. But today, steeling myself for Maddie leaving was enough and I couldn't muster up the energy to smooth things over, even if I'd been able to understand what I'd done wrong.

Neither of us spoke as we drove away. I pretended to be gazing out of the window, but I was trying to hide the tears pouring down my face. We stopped at the services near Sheffield for coffee, falling into the usual pattern of me finding a seat and Joel waiting for drinks. He shuffled about in the queue, radiating an irritation with everyone surrounding him, not stepping to the side so that a woman could squeeze past and swap her juice for water, shrugging his shoulders and mumbling to no one in particular as far as I could see.

It was a relief when we got home and we could both escape into our computers, competing to be the first to mutter about 'needing to check work emails'.

When Joel was in one of his critical moods, I'd learnt to let him get on with it. Our long marriage had taught me that he was often stressed about something else and giving him space to work through it usually led to him emerging a few hours later, lighter of spirit and opening a good bottle of wine by way of apology.

Tonight, though, that was clearly not the case. Despite my determination not to pander to his grumpiness when, for once, I felt as though I had first dibs on an off day, I cooked sea bass for him – a recognisable peace offering in our relationship. But he pushed it around the plate, jabbing at it half-heartedly with his fork without even bothering to pick up his knife. He sat side-ways to the table and looked for all the world as though he'd prefer to be in front of the TV with a tray to avoid the excruci-ating experience of dinner punctuated not by conversation but by cutlery scraping on crockery, death by a thousand tines. I hoped Maddie's absence wasn't going to turn every mealtime into an ordeal.

I stopped eating. 'Joel, is something wrong? I mean, really wrong? Beyond you being a bit sad at saying goodbye to Maddie?'

'Not really. Well, sort of.' He frowned and stared at his plate. When he looked up, he said, 'I didn't want to do this today.'

'What?' Terminal diagnoses, gambling addictions, redun-dancy flitted into my head.

'I think we should separate.'

I didn't think I'd heard right. I started to laugh in that snuffly, hysterical way that follows a bout of intense crying. 'Separate, what, as in divorce?'

Joel scratched at the fish skin on his plate. 'I can't do this any more. Maddie has hundreds of possibilities ahead of her while what lies ahead of me is more of the same – ensuring rich companies get even richer – until I retire. Going to Cornwall for one week with your mum, having a fortnight in Majorca in the summer, and all I have to look forward to in between is us weighing up the pros and cons of new programmes on Netflix.'

'The way you say that makes me feel like I'm the most boring person on earth.' I could hear the pleading in my tone, the desire to have him dismiss my words, to declare that he didn't think that at all. But if anything, he agreed with me.

'I think we've got into a rut. We both had a lot more energy, and much more fun, when we first met. We never wanted to stay in at the weekend if there was a chance to socialise.'

I couldn't process the conversation quickly enough. I wanted to argue, point out that he wasn't exactly a laugh a minute, not to mention that I couldn't remember the last time he had made me feel special. But confusion obscured any reasoning. The articulate army I needed to defend myself, to force him to be specific about what he meant, had scattered. 'So, that's it, you want to get a divorce without any discussion about what we could change, what we could do to move ourselves to a better place?'

Joel put his knife and fork together. I brushed away the thought that I could have saved myself the trouble of cooking. 'We've got so bogged down in raising Maddie – I mean, you've been a great mum – but it's been at the expense of us as a couple. I'm not sure we've had an exchange in years about anything other than Maddie's schoolwork and university applications, let alone all the palaver around selling your mum's house after your dad died. When was the last time we went out for dinner during the week or to see a band at the weekend?'

I felt as if I'd jumped into a freezing-cold sea on a sunny day, my chest all tight as though I was struggling for breath, everything flailing within me to right myself. I eventually managed a choked, 'I didn't know you felt like that. Why didn't you say something?'

Joel made a noise that felt both disparaging and desperate. 'I didn't think you'd make us a priority. It felt selfish to say I wanted your attention when you were so thinly stretched already.' He shook his head. 'When we were first married, you'd be straight up on the dance floor, always experimenting with your hair, dashing off to the beach as soon as it was sunny, filling the house with friends.' He paused. 'We're different people now.'

He was using the plural. Making it sound like a collective burden of failure. But really it was mine. The truth was that there hadn't been enough of me to go round and I'd assumed that the other grown-up on my team would be happy to take a back seat for a while – or step up and do some of the heavy lifting himself to free me up for the fripperies of wining, dining and dancing. The injustice of being criticised for doing my best for the whole family blindsided me.

'I don't think we are fundamentally different people, we just had such a lot of demands on us, one after the other – Maddie, helping Mum move. But it wasn't just my family. I had all that backwards and forwards to look after your parents when they were ill. I spent half my life on the motorway.' I was reeling from the unfairness of Joel holding against me all the occasions that I'd taken time off work to drive up to Derbyshire whenever his mum or dad had a health emergency, then later to sort out carers, repairs to the house, anyone who could keep his frail parents in their own home.

Joel looked affronted. 'So did I. I was up there nearly every weekend for months.'

I let it go. Even in these circumstances, it seemed mean to force him to accept the truth about his sporadic, resentful visits.

However, I hadn't given up trying to justify myself. 'Until the pandemic, I was commuting into London every day, then coming home to all the housework. It didn't leave me with much time for anything else. Someone has to do the boring stuff – cleaning, washing, cooking. Maybe if you'd helped out a bit more, I wouldn't have been so knackered.'

Joel's jaw tightened. I knew he was about to compete over who did what in the house. He would consider that he did his fair share precisely because he had no idea how much needed doing and how much happened without him ever being aware of it. But now wasn't the moment for that observation.

I reached for his hand. 'Please give us – me – another chance. Now I know how you feel, I'll make some changes. Mum's settled in her new flat, Maddie's leading her own life now—' I tried to keep the catch out of my voice. 'We can concentrate on what we want to do.' Reluctantly, I admitted to myself that I wasn't even sure what that might look like. I'd have to let Joel lead the way.

Joel pulled away from me. 'I'm sorry, Beth. You were so focused on Maddie leaving for uni that I didn't know how to start the conversation. You didn't have the headspace for it. A great opportunity has come up to lead a new project, so I've accepted a transfer to our Paris office.'

'What? When?' It began to dawn on me that this whole discussion wasn't an opening gambit, a testing of the waters to see how I reacted, but rather the presentation of a fait accompli, the announcing of the life he'd already planned without me. I fought to get my head around the fact that I was going from a family of three to living on my own. 'How long for? Is it a permanent move?' My voice was rising, panicky.

'I'm moving out there in a couple of weeks. The initial stages of the project should take between seven and eight months. It should finish about mid-May. You know I've wanted to go and live abroad for a while.'

Had I known that? Had he shared this burning desire to live in Paris, while I nodded absentmindedly, my attention on Maddie and her history revision or making sure I didn't burn the chicken in the oven? If he had articulated it, I'd probably assumed it was a passing fantasy. I was winded, my gaze flitting around the room, settling on our wedding presents – the pine coffee table, the clay jug, the dainty china cups that I'd displayed on a shelf because they only held two gulps of tea. All this stuff we'd hung onto despite only mildly liking it back then and positively hating it now. There'd be no argument over any of it. But this wasn't about our division of assets. I didn't want to separate. I wanted to show him that we – I – could recapture vibrancy, a sense of fun and adventure. I'd been that person once. Maybe I could be again.

'Joel, don't give up on our marriage. Go to Paris if you must, but promise me you'll give us a chance to make some changes before we do anything more permanent. I hear what you're saying. I'm sorry, I got overwhelmed by family life. But I will be better. Now I've got more flexibility with Maddie away.' I leaned forward, my eyes searching his. 'Please.' I didn't say out loud what I was thinking: *Don't let the next thing we tell Maddie be, 'Hope you're eating properly and not hitting the vodka too hard. Oh, not much has been happening here. Just Dad and I getting a divorce.'*

I couldn't let that happen.

Without much conviction, Joel muttered, 'Until the middle of next May then. But I'm not putting my life on hold. I'm fifty-two. My dad died at seventy-seven. That's another twenty-five years if I follow the same path. I don't want to waste it.'

My head was reeling. My own husband didn't want to squander his life on me. I was afraid of the answer to the next question but I couldn't not ask.

'What's the definition of "not putting your life on hold"? Other women?'

He shrugged. 'I'm not going to go looking for anyone. I'd like to stay married, in the right circumstances.'

He was so matter of fact, as though everything he said was obvious to anyone with a modicum of intelligence. As though throwing our marriage vows onto a footing of maybes and 'if nothing better turns up' was the most normal thing in the world, while pain scorched through me.

I rushed out the words. 'I'll pull myself together. I had no idea you were so unhappy. Please promise me that you won't go off with anyone else. Give me a chance to sort myself out.'

'I'll do my best. I don't want us to split up either, but I can't live like this any more.'

I was so scared of pushing him into ending our marriage right then and there, I murmured my agreement.

As he went into the sitting room and the news blared out, I sat rigid with shock. I hardly dared breathe in case the hurt that was lodged in my chest erupted in a burst of noise I couldn't control and finished Joel off completely.

2

In the weeks after Joel's departure, I dragged myself to the office, working from home as often as possible until my manager commented that 'working from home is a privilege, not a right.'

Despite my friend Helen, who occupied the next desk along, saying, 'You all right? You're very quiet' on a regular basis, I'd batted her off, using adjusting to an empty nest as an excuse for my low mood. I didn't intend to tell anyone that Joel had left me. I hoped that I could somehow miraculously transform into a glitteringly fascinating version of myself in the thirty or so weeks available to me and that he could seamlessly come back home without anyone outside of the household having to know that he'd gone AWOL. I couldn't stand the idea of everyone whispering about us and watching our every move on any social occasion. 'He walked out on her for a few months, you know.' 'Not looking good, is it? He can't bear to be near her.'

I'd pleaded with Joel not to tell Maddie over the phone. I wanted her to be totally carefree for these first few months, without the distant cloud of duty threading through her days, the background pressure to phone me, check on me, be interested in my life. And so far, I'd got my wish. There'd been the occasional FaceTime squeezed into the five minutes before she was disappearing to the Students' Union when I'd be granted a view of an arm or the top of her head as she put her make-up on or painted her nails. Now and again, she'd tack a 'What's happening with you?' onto the very end of the conversation, but more often than not, a noisy posse would be crowding into her room and the only possible answer was 'Everything's fine here, same old, same old' before I lost her attention and we shared a hurried goodbye.

But about two weeks before Christmas and two months after Joel had staggered out to his car with all his shirts falling off their hangers, Helen turned up at my door one Tuesday evening with a bottle of wine. 'Right, you can tell me to get lost, but I'm worried about you. Are you on your own or is Joel in?'

I shook my head, opening my mouth to lie about where he was. Instead, the words rushed out. 'He's left me.'

Helen stepped inside and shut the door. 'What? Why?'

I ushered her through to the sitting room and fetched some glasses and a bowl of nuts. 'I think the basic reasons are that I'm dull and boring and that he thinks that staying with me condemns him to a tedious old age.'

'He said that? In those exact terms?' She opened the bottle and poured our drinks.

I'd deliberately tried not to think about his words. 'He didn't put it quite like that, but that was the general gist. To be fair, he didn't say it was all my fault, but the bottom line is he wants more excitement and he doesn't feel that I'm likely to provide it.' I took a large gulp of wine. 'The trouble is I'm at such a low ebb, I don't really have the energy to start throwing myself into a load of new hobbies that will make me more interesting. It's all I can do to get through the day at work without sobbing in the loos.'

Helen scooped up a handful of peanuts. 'Are you sure this isn't all a big smokescreen? That he isn't seeing someone else?'

'Joel? No. Well, I suppose anything is possible, but he sounded more like he was having a midlife crisis, wanting to experience lots of things before it was too late. You know, the usual stuff: travel, eating out, going to concerts. And in some ways, I get it. I probably have become staid and inward-looking. It sort of crept up on me, all the years of putting Maddie first, then looking after both sets of parents. Booking holidays seemed like an extra stress over the last few years – not knowing whether one of them would suddenly get rushed into hospital and we'd have to cancel everything, plus all the COVID restrictions. I suppose I got a bit lazy.'

'So, do you want him back?'

Her tone suggested that I had some say in the matter, that I had a choice. I clung onto the idea that there might be hope.

'Yes. I can't bear the thought of telling Maddie that we're splitting up. She might even side with him. She's been nagging me for ages to buy some new clothes and to have some highlights so the grey hairs aren't so noticeable in the blonde.'

Helen scrabbled in her handbag for a pen. 'We'd better make a plan then.'

'What kind of a plan?' I asked, grateful that someone else might provide a pointer for a sensible way forward when all the nights I'd lain awake had failed to deliver.

'Well, as far as I can see, Joel has assumed that he can disappear off and you will dutifully sit here, caretaking the house and reading articles about how to become an interesting wife. The best way to play him at his own game would be to go off on your own adventure.'

I stared at her. Getting the train to London threw me into a tizzy of checking that my ticket hadn't somehow leapt out of my bag between leaving home and arriving at the station. I was embarrassed to admit that, so I offered up something that felt within the realms of achievable but still terrified me. 'I suppose

I could go on one of those holidays for single women. I've always fancied walking in Andalusia.'

Helen smiled. 'I was thinking about something more radical. Taking a sabbatical and going to live abroad, for example.'

'A sabbatical? What would I do for money? Where would I go?'

Helen frowned as though I was coming up with trifling objections to her grand plan. 'Beth, a week hiking around Seville or planning a couple of nights out isn't going to bowl Joel over. You need to do something completely out of character that makes him sit up and think, "Well, that's a side to Beth I didn't know existed." Who knows, you might even decide that you don't want him after all.'

I sat in silence, torn between endeavouring to come up with a proposal so daring that Helen's eyes would fly open and she'd say, 'Steady on now, I was only thinking of a fortnight's trek in Machu Picchu' and the reality that when we went on a week's holiday to Greece, I stressed about whether I'd packed enough sun cream and what we'd do if our passports were stolen.

'I wouldn't know where to begin.' I tried to make a joke. 'Maybe I should google how to become wildly thrilling so my husband loves me again.' My voice snagged. The gulf between how I'd imagined this stage of life now Maddie wasn't at home – Joel and I driving to the seaside, having brunch at the beach, last-minute weekends in the Cotswolds – and the reality of finding myself so lacking after all these years made a cold panic rise in my chest.

Helen topped up our glasses. 'You could start by going on one of those retreats that help divorced women work out their next steps.'

I wanted to cry then. 'I don't want to get divorced.'

Helen flapped her hand at me. 'No, of course not. But it might be useful, psychologically, to give you the confidence to know that you can survive anything, if things don't work out with Joel.'

There was a bit of me that was still waiting for Helen to rant about how Joel was mad to leave me rather than this rather insulting acceptance that he had a point and it was up to me to be different. Though I could understand her view that surprising him with a couple of tickets to a Rod Stewart concert might not be the reinvention that was required. I loved Rod, though.

Helen pulled her iPad out of her handbag. 'Let's just see what's out there.' She started to laugh. 'Oh look, a newly divorced bucket list. "Buy yourself a pair of impossibly high stilettos."'

Helen was starting to get on my nerves with her emphasis on divorce.

'Definitely not.' I even put insoles in my slippers. There was absolutely no way I was tottering about in some stupid heels and risking making a fool of myself by falling flat on my face.

'Go to a really posh nightclub in London.' Helen looked up expectantly. 'That would be a laugh. I'll come with you.'

'Absolutely not. I hated clubs when I was in my twenties. One of the most glorious things about having Maddie was thinking that now I was a mum, I would never have to go near a nightclub again.'

Helen shrugged. 'Spoilsport.'

'I don't think I can become someone else entirely,' I said, feeling hurt that Helen's attempts to help were cementing in my mind that I was death to all merriment.

'Let me google something else. How about "reinventing yourself in middle age"?' She tapped away on the screen. She did have very nice nails. I never found the time to file mine, let alone paint them with bright red polish. 'This is more up your street. It's an advert in *The Lady* of all things. Crikey. I'd like to do this myself. Look.'

She thrust the iPad towards me. I scanned the headline of the link she'd clicked on. *Suffered a traumatic event? Lost the joy in life? Want to remember what it was like to wake up every morning with wonder in your heart?*

I read on about an apartment that was available for a nominal rent to a British woman 'of a certain age'. There was a bit about the owner of the apartment, Veronica – 'Ronnie' – who, at seventy-four, held tight to the philosophy that there was always pleasure to be found, whatever the circumstances, and that it was an affront to the gift of life not to approach every day with joy. Her overall premise was that the world bumps and bruises us, but if we stay open to beauty and possibility, there was always happiness to be found and there was no better place to make that happen than Rome.

I glanced down the conditions, ready to brush off Helen's enthusiasm. Number one was that the applicant had to be at some sort of crossroads in life, through loss, relationship break-down or 'a significant change in circumstances' that had robbed her of her get-up-and-go. I could just about tick all three on that basis. Number two was that the person was to commit to staying for at least two and a half months. Number three was that she would agree to undertake a list of challenges to encourage her to change her mindset and how she viewed both the past and the future.

I tapped the screen. 'What challenges? I bet it's some weird scam – why would a stranger offer an apartment in the centre of Rome for a peppercorn rent to someone they'd never met? Either that or you'd end up being a skivvy for a woman who wants a live-in housekeeper but doesn't want to pay for one.'

Helen frowned. 'Don't be so negative. I think it sounds like a brilliant opportunity. Look, why don't you at least email her and find out a bit more?'

I picked up the now-empty wine bottle and took it into the kitchen. 'Absolutely not. How do I know that I wouldn't get out there and end up as a glorified cleaner living in a broom cupboard or, at the other end of the scale, forced to abseil down St Peter's dome? Nope. I'll find something closer to home, thanks.'

Helen trailed after me, puffing out her lips as though I was a hopeless case. A surge of anger rushed through me. Most fifty-year-old women didn't have to fly about the globe renting apartments in random cities and undertaking ridiculous trials to prove that they were worthy of their husbands' love in order to avoid staring down the barrel of loneliness. Thank goodness Maddie would be home in a week's time and would bring a bit of energy and noise to my empty house. My heart did a little twist at having to explain that Joel wasn't intending to come back from Paris for Christmas. So far, we'd told her he was out there on a work project for a few months and she'd been far too wrapped up in her new life to ask many questions. But I wasn't going to lie to her all holiday. Judging from his 'Tell her whatever you think is best – let me know what you decide', he wasn't about to volunteer to be the bad guy and break it to her that we might split up. A tiny part of me was clinging onto the idea that Joel might surprise me a couple of days before Christmas, realise that women my age might not be doing the shuffle dance on TikTok and crowd surfing at concerts but that didn't mean that we couldn't offer a happy and stable home.

Suddenly, weariness overwhelmed me. I wanted Helen to go, to leave me alone to be dreary without pretending to be any different.

Helen must have sensed my change in mood because she became all conciliatory. 'Well, we can look at things you could do in the new year. I'd best make a move now, got a meeting with that new woman in HR tomorrow.'

I waved her out, wondering how one minute it seemed perfectly acceptable to go to work, have dinner and watch a bit of TV and the next I wasn't meeting expectations unless I jetted off to a foreign city to engage in a stranger's bizarre experiment.

I was going through my nightly routine, double-checking all of the doors, peering out into the street for imaginary criminals who preyed on women living on their own when my mobile rang. Maddie.

'Are you all right?' I asked, my voice high with anxiety.

There was music in the background as though she was in a bar. My mind leapt to her calling to say her drink had been spiked, that she was stranded in the middle of nowhere and her friends had deserted her. Instead, a slightly irritable 'Yes, I'm fine, why?' buzzed down the phone against a backdrop of shrieking laughter.

'Well, it's quite late and you don't usually ring at this time.'

'We didn't go out until ten.'

Ten! What time would she be going to bed? With a force of iron will, I gobbled down my warnings about not getting run down or falling behind in lectures.

'It's lovely to hear from you.'

'Yeah, anyway, I was ringing to see if you and Dad mind if I don't come back for Christmas? Genevieve's parents have invited me to stay at their chalet in the French Alps. They run a ski business and one of the chalet girls has broken her leg so Gen and I are going to help out for the next four weeks. And I'm going to learn to snowboard!'

I sat down on a kitchen chair. I longed to sob that the only thing that had been keeping me going was the thought that she'd be home soon and I'd have a focus for my nurturing. That I'd been dreaming of snuggling up on the sofa with her and the Quality Street and watching all the cheesy Christmas films.

I tried to buy myself time. 'How well do you know Genevieve?' It made my heart ache to imagine Maddie at a table, laden with rustic decorations and candles and frivolity, raising a glass to someone else's mum, conversation bouncing around the room, their faces pink and shiny from a morning on the slopes.

'She's in the flat below me. She's on my course.' Maddie's voice held a note of impatience, as though I was focusing on entirely the wrong details. 'The thing is, I need to book my flight tomorrow because there aren't many seats left.'

I couldn't say no. I wanted her to embrace every experience offered to her. Wasn't spontaneity the holy grail of being an exciting and interesting person? Hadn't I been the one telling her to seize every chance that came her way? 'Of course you must go. Sounds like a fantastic experience.'

Her voice softened. 'You'll be all right with Dad and Nan, won't you? I'll ring you on Christmas Day.'

'I'll be fine, darling. Keep in touch. Anyway, it's late, I'm off to bed.' I cut the call quickly, before my neediness could leak out and take the shine off her pleasure.

I laid my head on the table and cried with the intensity of someone gathering up every disappointment, every hurt, every failure and distilling them into an acute and vocal agony. And a long time later, when my eyes resembled bloodshot lychees and my heart felt as empty as the December sky, I googled the details for 'Ronnie'. With everyone changing around me, I had no choice to keep up or be left behind. I tossed and turned all night, experimenting with different versions of myself to convince her that, of everyone who might apply, I was not only the person in the direst need but also the most driven to succeed.

3

The email came at the beginning of January to say that I'd been successful, that, in Ronnie's words, I'd convinced her 'that under the layers of duty and drudge, there was a youthful spirit ready to be unleashed'. I immediately wanted to write back and say, 'I can't do this, I'm not the sort of person who ups and leaves.' Instead, I told myself that I had eight weeks to get organised before the date she'd suggested in March and that plenty of retired people took off on holiday for months at a time.

I texted Joel, a bald little message that I deliberated over for days, the right combination of intrigue and cooperation. *I've taken a sabbatical from work and I'm moving to Rome at the beginning of March. I feel that we need to have a conversation with Maddie, rather than keep pretending that everything's okay and we're both just travelling or working away. Do you want to come home and we can do that together?*

I also wrote, *I've contacted the house insurers and arranged special insurance as the house will be empty for more than thirty days*, then deleted it. Let him think that I was a woman existing on a higher plane of admiring architecture and seeking out sunny bars for platters of prosciutto washed down with red wine, too carefree to consider trivial matters of house insurance.

Satisfyingly, it had the desired effect. He rang me within ten minutes.

'You're going to Rome? Why? Why Rome? How long for?'

Hearing his voice for the first time in weeks made me want to burst out with, 'Come home. Let's forget this nonsense. We can resolve this. We don't need to be competing for adventure one-upmanship'.

I forced myself to adhere to Helen's instructions: 'Make him feel as though he's on the back foot, that he's made a huge error of judgement, that you've realised that he's not the be-all and end-all, either.'

I ignored the desperate longing for Joel to articulate the words that meant I wouldn't have to be brave, wouldn't have to disappear off to Italy to prove my worth as a wife. I said, 'I've got nothing to keep me here at the moment. Fancied a change of scene and Rome is supposed to be amazing in the spring. You were quite right about recapturing our zest for life.' I wondered if I'd gone too far. I wanted him to feel that I'd stopped being a done deal, but not so much that he gave up the fight. I pulled the focus back onto Maddie, onto the family we'd created together. 'Anyway, I'd like to present a united front to Maddie, and explain that we both need a bit of time apart but that doesn't mean we're necessarily heading towards divorce.' There was a silence on the end of the line. I rushed in with, 'What do you think?' before he could contradict me and I would have to face the reality that, Rome or no Rome, my marriage was over.

'I think it's better if you tell her on your own. You don't have to high drama it.' I could picture him shrugging with his one free shoulder, the other trapping his mobile against his ear.

I wanted to object that I never high drama'd anything. On the contrary, I usually went along with everything. But arguing

the point would have played straight into the view he appeared
to have that I made a mountain out of every molehill. I opted for
studied nonchalance.

'Shall I say we're having a trial separation for a few
months?' I asked.

'Yes, say that we're seeing how it goes and we'll make a firm
decision before summer. I'll get in touch after you've spoken to
her and arrange for her to come out to Paris at some point.'

I longed to probe, 'Which way are you leaning at the
moment?' but the rush of worry about how Maddie would take
our news and whether I would deliver it in the right way
crowded out that question.

I couldn't understand Joel not wanting to come back, to
reassure Maddie that she was still totally and utterly loved and
that wherever either of us lived in the world, she was our main
priority. No. His parenting appeared to distil down to inviting
her over 'at some point'.

All my hope that Joel would step in during February and invite
me to Paris rather than stand by while I moved to Rome came to
nothing. So, reluctantly and nervously, on the first day of
March, I was at the airport trying to quell my rising panic as the
minutes ticked down to saying goodbye to Maddie, who'd
insisted on waving me off despite my concerns about her driving
after an emotional farewell.

After her initial bemusement that her dad and I weren't
one indistinguishable entity, lumped together until the end of
time, the anger had set in. 'You're both so selfish. Why would
you break up the family because you're a bit bored?' My
determination not to paint Joel as the bad guy was shrivelling
like a piece of cling film in the microwave. I had narrowly
managed to hang onto my prepared line of 'people change as
they get older and sometimes they need some time apart to

appreciate what they have'. I didn't want her to hate him. I hoped we'd be able to return to our family life, newly invigorated, wiser but unresentful, once Joel's stint in Paris was over. But, as luck would have it, when I told her I was intending to go abroad for a few months on my own, any fury she had felt towards Joel was immediately redirected towards me.

'Dad's gone to Paris for work. You're *choosing* to disappear to Italy. What if I want to come home for a weekend?' I had pointed out that she hadn't even returned for Christmas so she couldn't really expect me to put my life on hold on the off-chance she might visit for two days a term. She'd snorted in a 'That's entirely different' sort of way, which produced a dual reaction of resentment that chasing off abroad was fine for Joel but not for me, and guilt, because, well, that seemed an integral part of motherhood.

But as my leaving date had approached, I'd sensed that she had moments of feeling proud that I was doing something out of the ordinary. I even persuaded myself that I was setting her a good example, showing her that you didn't need to wait for a man to come with you.

'Will I be able to pop over?' she'd asked.

I'd told her to let me suss it out first, but if the owner was amenable, I'd love to have her to stay. 'Worst-case scenario, darling, we'll get a hotel for a few nights.' I'd allowed myself a quick daydream about shepherding her around Rome, pointing out the best cafés for coffee, confidently ordering in Italian at a family trattoria where they knew me by name.

On departure day, however, now that I had to hug my daughter and head off into the unknown, I felt as though I was emigrating to Australia and would never see her again. I dispensed with the brave face I'd held rigid all the way to the airport. We sobbed and clung to each other, punctuated with great wet bursts of hysteria. Despite me not wanting to release

Maddie, there was no chance of my tears drying up until she was out of sight.

I finally took control. 'Right. You come and visit me at Easter. No excuses,' I snuffled into her hair. 'I don't know why we're getting ourselves in such a state. I'll probably decide it's all been a terrible mistake and be back next week.'

As I said the words, Helen's voice echoed in my mind, her constant variations of 'Don't you talk like that. Think positive!' She was only trying to inspire me with confidence, but over the last couple of months since I'd made the decision to go to Rome and agreed a sabbatical with work, it was like being in the company of a relentless positive-thinking app. Every time I expressed any doubt about what I was doing, she'd roll out some fridge-magnet wisdom. 'The only person who can stop you achieving your potential is yourself.' 'You get to choose – glass half-empty or glass half-full.'

Sometimes I ached to sink to the floor and allow myself a full-on panic about whether a pipe would burst in the house in my absence. Or whether Maddie and her mates might come back from uni and have a party that would get out of hand because someone posted it on Instagram. Or if the woman they'd brought in to cover for me at work would be so brilliant that no one would want me back... Not to mention exactly how lonely I was going to be in Rome, where I knew precisely no one and only had a rusty grasp of Italian from when I'd worked a season on a campsite in Lake Garda, over thirty years ago. At least mobile phones and Google Translate had been invented now.

Yet, after all the doubts, all the soul-searching, all the anxiety, here I was, on my own, in a foreign country where I was going to sink or swim. Thankfully, after the initial fluster of brushing away the dodgy drivers touting for business at the airport and finding the official queue, anticipation about the adventure ahead was blossoming. Whenever my nerve faltered,

I kept repeating, 'So, Joel, look at your wife now. Not quite as dull as you thought.' And suddenly the dome of St Peter's was there on the skyline.

'The Vaticano?' I asked, triggering the taxi driver to hold what I assumed was a monologue about the beauty of the museums. I grappled to catch every tenth word and felt like an international polyglot when I managed a '*Splendido*' in the right place and the driver nodded vigorously and repeated it back to me.

We drew up at some magnificent wrought-iron gates, I paid the driver, stepped out with my suitcase and pressed the button on the intercom. I was expecting a voice honeycombed with age, but the '*Pronto?*' that reached me, then 'Beth! You're here. Come on in!' had all the hallmarks of vitality and vibrancy, as well as the warmth that had come across in Ronnie's patient responses to my emails.

The gates swung open and I dragged my case up a cobbled drive, where I was welcomed by a mimosa tree heavy with fluffy yellow flowers exuding their exotic fragrance. I thought briefly of the paltry collection of snowdrops and crocuses heralding the slow start of spring back home as I surveyed the irises, palms and camellias already waving goodbye to winter. Huge urns of bright pink geraniums flanked the top of a grand stone staircase where a taller than average woman, in loose turquoise harem pants, stood. Her grey hair was cut close to her head, with some of the feathery layers tipped with blue. She reminded me of Annie Lennox. She hurried down the steps in a way that made me want to say, 'Careful, no rush!'

There was none of that English reserve about her. She threw her arms around me with such vigour that I wanted to rear up and create a little distance between us. 'Brilliant you're here. This is going to be such an adventure. You're going to love everything Rome can teach you.'

I felt my anxieties recede at her focus on the city, my fears of becoming an unpaid skivvy fading. A little dog came trotting out and jumped up. 'I hope you like dogs. This is Strega. She doesn't realise she's not human, so she'll probably assume she's coming with you when you go out of the gates. Just push her back in. She won't bite.'

'She won't be a problem to me. I love dogs.'

Ronnie's face relaxed into the satisfaction I'd noticed before with dog owners. The recognition that you were part of their tribe, not an outlier who couldn't see the charm of a four-legged friend. It was definitely a shortcut to her warming to me.

She grasped my upper arm. 'Come on, we'll make that husband of yours sit up and take notice, you see if we don't. Let me show you to your apartment. You can settle in and then you'll come and have an aperitif with me.' She pointed to a large semicircular balcony and I took in the majesty of the ancient building for the first time, with its terracotta tiles and yellow, limewashed facade. I turned my attention back to Ronnie as she carried on. 'My daughter tells me off for being un-eco-friendly, but I've got one of those patio heaters. We'll have half an hour outside watching all the lights twinkling in Rome. Hopefully by the end of your stay, we'll be able to sit out there without them.'

My stomach lurched at how long ten weeks might seem once the initial thrill of being here had given way to the day-to-day reality of surviving in Italy by myself. I was already sensing that Ronnie was a woman used to getting her own way. It was a long time since I'd been terrified to turn down an aperitif. I dreaded to think what challenges – 'nothing too taxing' – she had in store for me.

I trailed after her up the stone steps, the tread worn and dipping in the centre. She led me through a huge wooden door with a knocker made from a giant iron hand. I had the sense of being a tiny cog in a whole wheel of history, of all the good and bad news, births and deaths, tragedies and celebrations that these majestic old walls had witnessed. She marched into a hallway lit by a huge chandelier, while I puffed behind, hauling my luggage. She pointed to a door on the left. 'That's my apartment. Because the palazzo is built into a hill, it's a bit of an odd layout. I've got my living quarters on this first floor and my bedrooms on the floor below.'

Halfway along the corridor, Ronnie produced a large brass key out of the folds of her trousers and unlocked a door tucked beneath a mosaic arch.

I followed her, straight into the sitting room, gasping at the elaborate fireplace with its marble pillars, the gold cornicing and polished parquet floor. 'It's stunning.' My mum would be delighted to hear I hadn't ended up in a backstreet slum and I couldn't wait to send pictures of my new abode to Maddie and Helen. And Joel, if the opportunity arose.

Ronnie nodded. 'Yes, it is. There are five apartments all together. Mine, and yours, on this floor, two on the next one and one right at the top where my friend Marina lives. My husband was an architect. He renovated this one just before he died.' She said it dismissively, as though it was something he'd knocked out in an afternoon. I wondered how long she'd been a widow. 'The other two are a work in progress. There might be a little noise from the plumbers while you're here, assuming I can find someone to install new bathrooms.' She led me through to the kitchen, a glorious bright space, with doors opening onto a terrace straight out of an Airbnb wishlist. She pointed to the fridge. 'I've put the basics in there for you – milk, water, cheese, ham... wine. And here's the espresso maker, you know how one of these works, don't you, simply fill the bottom with water and put it on the gas? Coffee's in here.' She looked at me. 'Please don't tell me you drink instant coffee?'

I shook my head, focusing on the times I got fancy with the cafetière on the rare occasions we had people to dinner, rather than the jars of Nescafé I'd donated to Maddie to take to university. Ronnie was obviously a woman with very specific views. I felt a spark of panic at the thought of having to live up to yet another person's expectations, but there was no time to dwell on that.

'Aperitifs on my balcony in half an hour.'

As commands went, it was entirely bearable.

4

The next morning, I woke up totally disorientated, lying in bed for a few minutes, my eyes flickering from the elaborate ceiling rose to the promise of sunlight beyond the shutters. I forced myself to feel excited, wishing I had more inclination to leap out of bed and rush around, shouting, 'Let the adventure begin.'

As instructed by Ronnie, I decided to adopt the habit of not doing anything before I'd had coffee. I wandered out onto the terrace, testing the temperature. I settled down with my cup in a sheltered corner, marvelling at the fact that it was so mild, I didn't even need my dressing gown. However nerve-wracking the day ahead, I couldn't resist feeling a bit smug as I turned my face to the warmth rather than chipping the ice off my wind-screen back home before I could drive to the station. I dipped a brioche into my coffee and leaned back, savouring the sun on my skin before spoiling the moment by wondering how strong the rays had to be before I needed to whip out my factor fifty.

I was considering whether a second coffee might send me into overdrive when voices from Ronnie's terrace drifted over. 'Well? What was she like? Don't tell me. Let me guess. She was wearing a plain baggy T-shirt, a pair of comfortable trousers, a

jacket with no waist or shape, no jewellery apart from her
engagement and wedding rings, her hair hasn't really got a style
and—' I didn't recognise the voice. English, yes, but with an
inflection, a rhythm slightly out of kilter.

'Stop it, Marina. Not everyone has five hundred necklaces
and spends twenty minutes every morning matching one to
their outfit.' That low, masculine tone was definitely Ronnie.
And with a jolt to my stomach, I realised that they might be
talking about me.

The first voice moved closer. 'For goodness' sake. Why are
English women so unstylish? We don't want her wandering
about telling everyone she lives here and looking like a scare-
crow. Everyone will think our standards are slipping in our old
age.'

A chair scratched across the terrace and I could only hear
the murmur of Ronnie's reply. I wanted to shout over that I'd
been wearing a fitted blouse not a baggy T-shirt and what sane
person didn't wear comfy trousers to travel in? Although, to be
fair, the Italian woman in front of me on the plane had worn a
fedora and fur bolero for the whole journey.

I decided not to feed my insecurities any further and crept
inside. I quashed the prickle of tears, telling myself that Marina
hadn't even seen me, let alone met me. But there was no
denying that some of her stereotyping was spot on. Was I really
so frumpy? I'd always prided myself on a simple, dependable
wardrobe. Mostly black. I didn't need to stand out at my age.
My main priority was keeping my upper arms covered – I
couldn't say when it had happened, but at some time in the last
few years, the skin on my upper arms had collapsed like a
soufflé taken out of the oven too soon.

I riffled through my wardrobe to locate something that
might pass muster. What had seemed 'capsule' and elegant at
home now seemed cheap and unstylish. Anyway, today I was

exploring the city and finding my bearings, so I didn't need to drag out my finery.

Ronnie had suggested I get the bus from outside the apartment, but the whole buying of tickets at the newsagent's beforehand and validating them on the bus sounded a bit complicated for my first day, so I'd decided to walk.

I debated over whether to ring Ronnie's bell on my way out. I wasn't entirely sure how much nannying she intended to do. She'd given me a map the night before and wiggled her fingers dismissively when I'd asked her to point out Piazza Navona, the Trevi Fountain, the Spanish Steps and the Colosseum. 'Obviously you have to see them – people would think you were mad if you came here and didn't. But you can visit those sights any time. We need to get started on our project as soon as we can. Two and a half months will fly by.'

I knew that I'd signed up to being a project, hence paying a paltry amount for an apartment six hundred yards from the Vatican, but I still baulked at hearing it out loud.

Ronnie had tapped the map. 'Right, the first thing you must do is learn to notice the beauty all around you. I could see from your email that you're so busy looking after everyone – your daughter, your husband, your mother – that you've forgotten what it's like to see the wonder in small things. So that's where we're going to start. You head to Giardino degli Aranci – the orange garden – it's not too touristy and the view is spectacular.'

My instincts were that Ronnie would expect me to be independent and I didn't want to come across as someone who needed spoonfeeding. She'd already explained where to go. I put my money belt on under my top and zipped my keys into my leggings.

I was just heading towards the gate when Ronnie leaned over her balcony. 'Beth! Morning. How are you?'

Another head bobbed up beside her, shoulder-length jet-black hair with a white Mallen streak, giving her the appearance of a glamorous headmistress.

'This is Marina. She lives in the apartment at the top.'

I waved, squinting in the sunshine. 'Hello! Nice to meet you.'

Marina called down. '*Piacere*. Where are you going?'

I recognised the strident tone of her speech as belonging to woman I'd overheard earlier. I shouted up my proposed itinerary.

'No. No. No. Not like this. You cannot walk around the city in leggings. Only tourists wear gym clothes in the streets.'

I stood, craning my neck, stunned by the forthrightness of someone I'd only just met, bellowing sartorial rules down to me. All the confidence I'd squirrelled together to push myself out of the relative safety of Ronnie's apartment into a big city where I could barely speak the language evaporated. My eyes stung. Who would even be looking at me anyway? Surely in a metropolis such as Rome, people had better things to do than worry about whether my trousers were Lycra or linen?

Marina's head disappeared, and she emerged from the main doorway. She strode over to me, kissing me briskly on both cheeks. 'I'm Marina, half-Irish, half-Italian.' Before I could comment, she juggernauted on. 'Now, if I've understood well, you're here to rediscover yourself. Leggings are not the way to start.'

Marina's full-on barrage stopped my brain being able to function. I wanted to argue that I didn't want to rediscover myself. I wanted Joel to *rediscover his love* for me. I was here to teach my husband a lesson and to make myself so interesting that he would beg me to return. But with Marina directing me up to my apartment, all I managed to say in my defence was 'I'm only going for a walk.'

Ronnie joined us. 'She's so bossy, but you'll get used to her.

I couldn't stand her when I met her forty-five years ago, but she's grown on me.'

I'd never had a conversation that honest in my life. Maybe that was where I'd gone wrong.

Before I knew it, Marina was swiping through my wardrobe and I stood there, dumbfounded, caught between self-loathing as I pretended to laugh along and fury that at fifty I was letting myself be bossed around like this. Surely this couldn't be the 'Italian' way?

Marina pulled out a pair of black linen trousers and a plain T-shirt. 'These are the right things to wear for exploring. You have to dress like you respect yourself, otherwise no one else will. I know what you're thinking, that it's none of my business what you wear. And in a way, you are right. But you are here to make a change. Ten weeks is not so long. So, no leggings outside of these walls. You don't have to be all la-di-dah dressed up, but you should always be able to walk into any restaurant without the waiter looking down his nose at you. And always a jacket. It's too early in the year to go out without one.'

Ronnie said, 'I'm sorry, but this is Italy. People do judge you on what you wear.'

I all but snatched the clothes from Marina. 'All right. I'll change.' I added, 'If it's that big a deal,' to their retreating backs.

Moments later, I marched out of the house, my jacket tucked under my arm as a feeble act of rebellion without glancing up to see if they were leaning over the balcony, humiliation coursing through me.

The bus Ronnie had instructed me to catch raced past me and I took a childish satisfaction in disobeying her instructions. I pounded the pavement, barely taking in my surroundings through the fog of indignation until I turned left and found myself a couple of hundred metres from the huge square of St Peter's Basilica. Even from a distance, the beauty of the pillars, topped with a balustrade and statues, stopped me in my tracks. I walked to the centre, where I stood staring up at the dome, the sun glinting off the golden sphere perched on the top, feeling for the first time that I was really in Rome. That I'd made it. And, reluctantly, as I scanned the Italians striding through the square in their tailored trousers and thick woollen coats despite the sunny weather, I had to concede that I didn't stick out half as much as the tourists in their trainers, shorts and baseball caps. I had half a mutinous thought about not caring about 'fitting in', before I was instantly seduced by the idea of being mistaken for someone who lived in Rome permanently.

I tore myself away. It was a fifty-minute walk to the Giardino degli Aranci that Ronnie had directed me to and I was terrified of returning that evening with blisters but nothing to report. Time would tell whether Helen's conviction that 'getting out of your comfort zone in Rome is exactly what the doctor ordered'. Right now, I felt as though I had just invited more people into my life to disappoint.

I followed the river, not daring to deviate from the route despite the myriad interesting alleyways that invited a meander. I needed the satisfaction of telling Ronnie and that insufferable Marina that the first task they'd set me had been a piece of cake.

I steamed along, swerving around people on the pavement, none of whom bothered to say thank you, even when I did an exaggerated move to avoid them. Eventually, I crossed over the river when I got to the Isola Tiberina as instructed – 'You can't miss it, it's a little island in the middle of the river, with beautiful bridges linking it to the banks.' I found the next landmark, the big open space Ronnie had described, Circo Massimo, an ancient chariot-racing stadium. I finally managed to dodge through the traffic to some gates on the other side and scuttled self-consciously past the workmen gathered on the bench. They were eating lunches that put my supermarket meal deals firmly in the shade. One of them even had a cloth napkin.

My pace slowed with the lack of conviction that I should be

walking up a hill. No point in wearing clothes to blend in with the locals if I was permanently attached to Google Maps, walking twenty steps one way and then the same in the other direction in the hope that the blue dot would give me a heads-up. I was about to turn back when I saw an opening on the right.

Within a few moments, I was standing on a large terrace, with a handful of other tourists and the most glorious view over Rome. I sat down on the wall as a busker started to sing 'Here Comes the Sun'. They were exactly the words I needed to hear and, for the first time since I'd arrived, I felt my body dampen down the red alert pumping through my veins and relax into the music. Please let the sun both literal and metaphorical light up my world.

I tried not to wonder what Joel was doing and concentrated on the singer. I wanted to appreciate everything about the person who had no idea how much I needed to hear an anthem of hope in that moment. He was older than his voice suggested, maybe early forties, beautifully dressed, though why anyone would need a long leather jacket and scarf on a day like this was beyond me. I was sweating in a T-shirt, despite Marina's concerns about me freezing to death without a jacket. When he finished, I threw a coin into his cap. A cap in which any Englishman would look like Granddad Percy off to the allotment. He, however, would no doubt manage to position it on top of his long curly hair and carry it off with the special kind of grace that streamed through the Italian DNA.

He smiled. 'Thank you! Have a good day, *signora*.'

Not quite indistinguishable from the locals yet, then.

I missed Joel so much in that moment. Or maybe just that anchor of being in a couple, where I wasn't so vulnerable to other people's opinions. I was so tempted to text him. Our conversations leading up to my departure had been indignant and fraught. He'd clearly taken it for granted that I'd housesit the family home while he jaunted about Paris, all strolls along the Seine and sunset views of the Eiffel Tower. He had been outrageously put out that he'd had to pitch in to organise the logistics of keeping an empty house ticking over safely.

I wasn't going to fall at the first hurdle. Let him sweat.

I scrolled past his name but the ache to hear a familiar voice persisted. I rang Maddie instead, hoping I wouldn't be disturbing her in a lecture. I prepared my voice to be upbeat and chirpy.

'Mum! How are you? What's it like?'

I hadn't mentioned the challenges that were a condition of me being here. Somehow telling her I wanted to change made me feel as though I would be saying that I regretted all the compromises I'd made so I could be around for her. I filled her in on my apartment with its view over the Vatican, receiving a gratifying 'That sounds amazing' in response. I described Ronnie and made her laugh with my account of Marina throwing her hands up in horror about me going out in leggings. 'She should come and see me and my uni mates going to the corner shop for biscuits in our pyjamas.' Her finding it funny lessened the sting, making me feel as though, rather than an insult, it was a fun story to recount.

'Anyway, overall, it's surpassed my expectations. It's the first week of March and here I am sitting in an Italian park in the sunshine.' I felt a rush of pride. I was still wobbly, still terrified, but I'd come.

Abruptly, Maddie finished the call – 'Gotta go, Mum, they're all waiting for me, great you're having a good time'– and rushed off to her life, the one I wasn't part of any more. I was left savouring the bittersweet blend of wishing she was still little, depending on me for everything, juxtaposed with the joy of seeing her fly.

Reaching out for the touchstone of home made me restless. My satisfaction at regaling Maddie with my adventure was fluttering away, so I consulted the map and decided to move on to the other place Ronnie had instructed me to visit. A keyhole in a door somewhere, something to do with the Knights of Malta. I couldn't help wondering if Ronnie and Marina were somehow tracking me running around Rome, laughing that they'd dispatched a naïve Englishwoman to the other side of the city to squint through a keyhole. They seemed far too straightforward to play a silly prank like that, though.

I walked further up the hill until I reached a square with a few people lined up in front of a huge green door. A burst of relief shot through me that Ronnie wasn't sending me on a wild goose chase – or if she was, I wasn't the only one to fall for it. I joined the queue, watching people attempting to take photos through the keyhole. When I finally made it to the front, I gasped when I saw what they were looking at. St Peter's Basilica framed in the distance by an archway of hedging in the foreground. So perfect that I wanted to ignore the impatient fidgeting behind me and take a moment. Instead, I queued up again, unable to believe that someone had managed to line up a tiny aperture like that with a building three kilometres away.

I gathered the view to me like a squirrel storing acorns for winter. I'd done so little out of the ordinary over the last few years, and although it would be convenient to blame the pandemic, the truth was I'd stopped pushing myself to expand my horizons. And now, there were so many horizons to choose from and this unique panorama was just the beginning.

Emboldened, I decided not to walk back the same route I'd come, turning towards an area called Testaccio. If I could find somewhere that didn't look too intimidating, I'd stop for a coffee. At the very least, I'd get some exercise.

I took off down the hill, deliberately emptying my head of thoughts of home, of Joel, of Maddie. Before I'd gone more than a hundred metres, I heard footsteps very close behind me, which immediately made me hug my bag close to me.

'*Signora*, we meet again.'

I turned. It was the busker.

I smiled and said hello, waiting for him to scoot past with his guitar. Instead he slowed down.

'Where are you going?'

I immediately pretended to have a specific destination in mind as a pre-emptive block to whatever he wanted from me. 'I'm having a bit of fresh air before an appointment at my apartment.' I carried on walking as if to underline my urgency, hoping to sound less like a tourist and more like someone who had a jet-set life, residing for chunks of time in many exotic locations during the year.

He gestured to my bare arms. 'Summer is here already for you?'

I did then – of course – default to talking about the weather and how incredible it was to be able to sit outside at this time of year. And before I knew it, we were chatting about England. Just in case he was in the habit of tailing any woman who chucked him a euro, I said, 'My husband and daughter will be so jealous when I tell them how warm it is.' All the while, Joel's warning voice was sounding in my head. *You shouldn't encourage him by being friendly.*

Halfway down the slope, he said, 'Do you have time to come for a coffee with me?'

I started to do the whole, 'No, no, I really should be getting back', although I was finding him so entertaining with his stories about where he'd travelled and how he paid his way wherever he was in the world by picking up his guitar when he ran out of money. 'Pubs in London, parks in Barcelona, boulevards in Paris.' I wanted to ask if he needed a licence, if he'd ever got into trouble with the police, if he worried about not having a pension. Instead, I experimented with my new persona of being a woman who upped and left her whole life behind, as though I paid no heed to such bureaucratic trifles.

We reached the bottom of the hill. I hesitated, not wanting to advertise the fact that I had no clue where I was.

'I'll show you my favourite café. The best *panini con prosciutto e mozzarella,*' he offered.

It was daylight. There were tons of people about. My heart held a crumb of rebellion that wanted to stick two fingers up to Joel: *Look at me. You thought I'd be sitting at home with my Kindle and instead, I'm going for coffee with a very cool, very handsome Italian.* And my decision was made.

Rico, as he introduced himself, led me to a little café in a square, where he greeted everyone in the bar with handshakes and backslapping. I half-expected the waitress to eye me with suspicion or mouth a warning to me, but she was all smiles, waving us to a table outside.

Once our food and water arrived, Rico turned his attention to me, making me feel both self-conscious and interesting in a way I hadn't for years. On impulse, I'd told him my name was Elizabeth, to maintain some formality, even though only my mother called me that.

But my new friend wasn't having any of it. 'So, Elizabeth, I shall call you "Betta"; Elizabeth to me is so serious. I think you don't need such a serious name.'

'I'm a serious person,' I said, hoping he would think I was joking. 'But, actually, most of my friends do call me Beth.'

'You are serious. But I don't think you have to be.' He leaned towards me, and close up, I noticed the flecks of grey in his stubble. 'So, Betta, what are you doing in Rome? How long are you here? Why alone?'

I took a bite of the panino to give myself time to reply. I'd never see him again so I opted for a highly embellished half-truth, so far from the actual truth that I almost expected to see everyone's heads jerk round in the café. 'My daughter's started at university and I wanted to do something for myself. I don't see why the young should be having all the adventures. So I came in search of one of my own.'

I expected him to nod, impressed by my get-up-and-go, but instead he frowned.

'And your husband, Betta, he doesn't mind this?'

So much for a light-hearted exchange with the locals. 'It's not for very long, a couple of months. We've been married nearly twenty-five years, but we've always been independent. He's very supportive of the idea, just wants me to be happy.' I forced myself to inject conviction I didn't feel into my voice.

'So he sits at home earning the money, while you travel.' Rico tapped the side of his head. 'Clever woman.'

During the rest of lunch, I diverted him from further scrutiny of my marriage by asking about the must-see lesser-known things in Rome, then cursed myself for making it sound like I was asking him to show me around.

After he'd teased me about asking for a cappuccino, before allowing me a macchiato, I excused myself to the loo so I could look at Google Maps and plan how to get home. I returned to the table and pulled out my wallet.

'Ah no, no, no. This I offer you.'

'Let me at least pay my half.'

He pushed his dark curls away from his face. 'Betta. Stop being so English. It is my pleasure to buy you a sandwich. You offend me if you don't accept.'

I dithered between accepting and fretting that if I did, he'd somehow expect something in return. From a woman ten years his senior wearing orthotic insoles? I was probably flattering myself. But even if that wasn't an issue, I'd be concerned about whether I'd scoffed down his earnings for the day.

He took my hand, which turned the whole scenario up another notch of awkwardness. I wasn't naturally tactile, especially with people I'd just met. I had an unwelcome flashback to reaching out to hold Joel's hand on one of the last walks we'd taken together and his shaking me off, saying he was too hot. In September. In the drizzle.

I kept perfectly still, hoping my palm wasn't sweaty.

Rico put his head on one side as though he was really studying me. 'You looked sad when I was singing. This is supposed to be a happy phase for you, your big adventure. No one should be sad in Rome. We only have this one life, you know. Don't waste it.'

If Joel had been biding his time, waiting until he could ditch his deadwood wife, then perhaps I'd already wasted my best years. I stood up, freeing my hand, a rush of despair dragging at my insides. 'It's been lovely meeting you, Rico. I've got to go now.' I threw down some euros. 'Please let me treat you. Good luck with your music. And thank you for the company.'

He started to say, 'Wait, wait, let me at least show you the bus stop for the Vatican.'

I brushed him off, my fear of bursting into tears and making a scene outweighing my horror at being rude. I hurried to the end of the square and darted down a side street, asking myself what on earth I thought I was going to achieve by coming to Rome.

5

By the time I keyed in the code for the big gates to Villa Alba, I was not in the mood for Ronnie and Marina. My feet felt like melons neglected in the fruit bowl for far too long, ready to split open in a squidgy mess at the slightest provocation.

I managed to slip into my apartment without encountering either of them. I sat on the terrace, ashamed that despite my distant view of the Vatican, if I dug down deep into my heart, the thing I wanted most was to be in my own kitchen cooking Joel's favourite dinner – pork loin in a soy and garlic sauce – and agreeing to watch one of the gory detective box sets that he loved. But there was no more room for moping, because a knock on my door meant I had to plaster on the 'game for everything' face that had persuaded Ronnie to choose me in the first place.

Of course, she wanted a full report. I didn't invite her in and hoped she'd get the hint that I wasn't in the mood for a chat right now, but she leaned on the doorjamb, showing no inclination to move without giving me a thorough grilling. 'So did you speak to anyone? Have you tried out any Italian? What struck you as different from the UK?' I could feel something horribly like resentment rising in my chest as she asked for more and more details. I didn't want to be Ronnie and Marina's pet project, a little plaything to school until I came up with the right answers. However, I knew I'd have to throw her a few crumbs before she'd leave me alone.

Ronnie's eyes lit up when I told her about the busker. 'Oh brilliant! He can be one of your challenges. You need a romance with a totally unsuitable man. A love affair that's not going anywhere.'

I didn't even manage a jokey tone as I said, 'I think you've forgotten I'm here to get my husband back.' The insult that this woman was so dismissive of the thought that consumed nearly every minute of my day surged through my veins. I really was wasting my time here, but not for the reasons Rico thought.

Ronnie shrugged, seemingly nonchalant about the fact that she might have offended me. 'Oh don't be so serious. You don't have to take it anywhere. Why don't you go and learn to flirt again? The Italians are very good for that.'

I shook my head. I did not want to be having this conversation with someone old enough to be my mother. I had a retrospective appreciation for the way my own mum avoided asking too many questions in case she had to deal with an answer she didn't like. When I'd rung the previous evening to let her know I'd arrived safely, she had quickly curtailed our exchange when I'd shown a sign of veering beyond 'everything is absolutely fine on my wonderful adventure' by musing out loud about whether I was doing the right thing.

Ronnie was undeterred. 'Tell me that your busker friend didn't bring a frisson of romance with him? We are never too old for that little shivery feeling shimmering in our hearts.' I must have grimaced because she insisted. 'You know, that push/pull of wanting, because nothing says hope better and more loudly than love, and not wanting because' – she gestured to me, as though I epitomised the failure of love – 'every romance means we must ask ourselves, "Do I measure up? Do I meet this person's expectations?" And if we don't, we have to work out if the problem is theirs, or ours.' She pushed a blue-tipped strand of hair from her face. 'With the men I've known, it's always been their problem.' She threw back her head and laughed.

And despite my annoyance, I couldn't help but have admiration for her, for the fact, that, even in jest, she could voice those words out loud. With half of her confidence, I could have led a different life all together. I immediately countered that thought with the knowledge that I couldn't regret my marriage whichever way it went because I'd had Maddie.

I still hadn't invited her in, but Ronnie showed no indication that she was going anywhere. I had a pang of guilt at not allowing her into her own apartment, but this challenge nonsense was starting to feel like a huge mistake. Even if I left before my time was up, I'd have to stick it out for at least a fortnight after the big fanfare of telling everyone I was 'moving to Italy', purely from a pride point of view.

Ronnie murmured, 'We'll leave that challenge for later on.'

I ignored her. There was no way I was going on a date with anyone.

Just as I hoped she was winding up, Marina appeared in the hallway behind her and a swift exchange of news took place in Italian.

Marina let out what could only be described as a dirty laugh and clapped her hands. 'So. What else did you see on the way to Giardino degli Aranci and the keyhole? What things made your heart sing?'

I resigned myself to having to satisfy Marina's curiosity as well as Ronnie's but intended to fob her off with the bare minimum so I could put my feet up. 'I saw some lovely architecture. Lots of beautiful buildings. St Peter's Square is stunning.'

She clicked her tongue. Clearly I hadn't delivered the answer she needed. 'Yes, but everyone knows St Peter's Square. I mean things that other people rush past, that they don't take time to look at because they are too busy focusing on what they think is important.'

'I probably didn't absorb as much as I will in future because I was doing my best not to get lost en route to the gardens.'

Marina harrumphed, as though I was a parochial innocent abroad. 'So your next challenge is to find beauty in small things. We spend our entire lives obsessing about the big things, without realising that the little things matter more. Since you don't seem ready to get the bus yet, you should find it easy to discover them on foot. Shall we say roughly a week for this task, you report to us next Saturday?'

I ignored the implied disapproval that I hadn't tackled the bus and attempted to banish the feeling of a school girl standing in front of a teacher while she handed out assignments. 'What sort of things do you mean?'

'Anything that brings you joy,' Ronnie said.

And with that, she beckoned to Marina and turned on her heel, her long magenta scarf trailing behind her. I was left wondering how I'd been persuaded to leave my life behind to do the bidding of a woman whose motivations for having English women to stay in her apartment were not yet clear.

Sagging with the relief of not having to perform any more, I shut the door. I picked up my phone, my stomach still doing that little plummet of disappointment that there wasn't a message from Joel, even after five months of weaning myself off him. I opened a WhatsApp from Helen. *How's it going? Have you had to run through Rome naked yet?* complete with a GIF of someone eating their own body weight in spaghetti.

I phoned her, hoping she'd have some bright ideas about what on earth Ronnie meant by stuff that 'brings joy'. She sounded flustered. 'Sorry, I'm running round getting food for Ryan and his friends – a whole gaggle of them have just arrived from uni for the weekend. Can I call you later?'

I rang off, telling her that I was going to have an early night in an overly bright voice to disguise the wave of loneliness that was engulfing me. With three kids, her household was always so busy, so vibrant. If I'd had more than one child, or perhaps a son, maybe Joel might have been more invested in our family, if there'd been more going on. Or maybe not.

I took myself to bed, feeling as though everyone else had the answers to life. Even the busker with his hand-to-mouth existence of fifty-cent pieces tossed into a cap had a clearer idea than I did of his place in the world.

The next morning, I got up early and gave myself a stern talking-to about how lucky I was to have this opportunity and how I should stop worrying about what everyone else was doing and make the most of what I had right in front of me. I sat in the sun, with my coffee and decided to take Ronnie at her word. I would seek out joy and if my joy wasn't the same as hers, too bad. In fact, I'd show her that I wasn't the rule follower, totally lacking imagination, that she took me for.

I googled 'Unusual places in Rome that tourists don't usually see'. I flicked through the results and decided to go to Coppedè, which appeared to have some unique architecture. I'd have to get the bus. Ronnie could stick that in her pipe.

I crept out of the house, dreading that Marina was going to be on wardrobe-watch. I was disproportionately thrilled to have exited without encountering her. As I made my way across St Peter's Square to Piazza del Risorgimento, I felt the anticipation of discovery rather than the burden of dancing to someone else's tune that had dogged me the day before. I even managed to buy a travel ticket at the newsagent's kiosk. I was so proud of myself for locating the tram stop I needed. A pride that diminished five minutes later when the ticket inspectors got on and issued me with a fine for not validating the ticket in the machine. All eyes were upon me as I fumbled in my bag for my passport and handed it over, apologising and pulling out fifty euros, livid that I hadn't remembered Ronnie's instructions about the necessity of stamping it.

When the ticket inspectors finally left, an older woman looked me up and down, shook her head and muttered something about '*turisti*'. I tried to explain that I didn't know, that I'd made a mistake, but she pulled her lips into a sneery pout and, in that moment, I wanted to stick my finger in her face and shout about everything that had gone wrong for me.

I almost got off the tram then and there, but I reasoned that I'd already triggered everyone's disapproval, so I might at least get to where I was going. The Buenos Aires stop couldn't come quickly enough. I heaved a sigh of relief and headed to Piazza Mincio. There all my humiliation faded away, as I was transported into a fairy-tale square.

When I'd first moved to Purley, I'd often taken the train into London at weekends for the pleasure of wandering around posh Edwardian terraces, peering into the private squares around Kensington and Chelsea, losing myself in Hampstead Hill Gardens, nature and architecture nurturing my soul as a counterbalance to the long hours at my desk focusing on rows of figures. I tried to pinpoint why I'd stopped doing it. I supposed more pressing claims crowded out these little oases of relaxation. It was hard to believe that now I had no demands on me, no other goal than to spend time absorbing the magnificence of the buildings around me.

I had pangs of guilt, as though I should be doing something more useful, more productive, as I stood staring up at Palazzo del Ragno, so named for the huge spider over the door. The windows with their twisty masonry reminded me of something out of Hansel and Gretel. I ran my hands over the frogs spurting water in the square's fountain before sitting on the steps of an office with an elaborate shell-like entrance below several floors of rooms with pillared balconies. I envied anyone employed

there. But maybe they still got up on a Monday morning, pulled
a lasagne from the freezer, kicked a pair of trainers out of the
way and ran to the station, thinking, *Same old shit.*

I sent photos to Maddie. She responded immediately. *That
looks amazing! You're so cool doing this. Am gearing up for a
visit!* I nourished a little hope that Maddie would come out and
I'd be leaping on and off buses, leading the way with all the
authority of a proper tour guide. I wasn't even sure I was
allowed guests. I marvelled at my capacity to worry about the
details of the future when I hadn't even made it to the end of
the first week yet.

I took a few more photos of the spectacular archway, still
fixated on whether the people occupying the rooms with huge
windows overlooking the square floated about in a higher state
of bliss. Perhaps they existed in permanent fury that every time
they tried to enjoy their view, someone like me was snapping
pictures of their home.

I lingered in front of the mansions with their towers and
walls frescoed with ships, like something out of an enchanted
village, before taking a final picture of a wrought-iron gate that
was a sculpture in its own right. Twisted spiky metal, curls and
crowns to keep out intruders but done with such a blend of
functionality and splendour that the owners deserved never to
be burgled.

As I walked back to Villa Alba, I noticed how brilliantly the
Italians combined aesthetics with purpose. I stopped to examine
a cast-iron bin embossed with a relief of a she-wolf – one of the
symbols of Rome. Nothing like the utilitarian litter bins that
dotted Purley's streets. I made a mental note that when I went
back to England, I would never buy anything useful that didn't
also incorporate an element of beauty. Which, given that my
kitchen was full of glass storage jars and plastic baskets
designed to keep everything in order, gave me plenty to go at. I
recognised a moment of achievement, as though I'd understood

one tiny but vital thing. I might not understand how to hang onto my husband, but, my goodness, I was going to have the most visually pleasing house.

I crossed the gardens of Piazza Cavour, wanting to celebrate the tiny green shoot of happiness in my heart. Reluctantly, I acknowledged that Marina might have a point about the little things being the big things. I debated plucking up enough courage to order coffee on my own. The cafés around the periphery looked a bit daunting, with the tables of office workers jabbering and laughing away. But I had to get used to doing things by myself in case that was to be my permanent lot in life. I gazed around for a distraction to block that train of thought, my attention landing on a woman about Maddie's age, who wheeled her bike over to a bench and rummaged about for her book. She lay out flat, using her rucksack as a pillow, her book shielding her eyes from the sun. I was transfixed by how carefree she appeared, settling down without even glancing around, comfortable in her own skin. I wanted to be her. To be that person with the freedom to stretch out to read in a Roman piazza, with all my life still ahead of me, no wrong turnings, not yet so boring that I'd get dumped like yesterday's picnic.

And with that image in mind, I spent the next few days walking for hours, with no fixed destination, simply strolling down any alleyway or street that took my fancy. Rome was theatre in itself – the driving, the gesturing, the unexpected. And while I took photos of pillars, courtyards and skylines, I mulled over Ronnie's advice about getting a few lessons on learning how to flirt so I could put the skills to use with my own husband. For the moment, however, I would tell myself that an eventual return trip to the Giardino degli Aranci was to admire the statues, arches and windows that I'd raced past before. Beauty in small things. But also in singing Italians.

6

On Friday, the day before I was to meet Marina and Ronnie to
report back on the week's challenge, I set off for Trastevere, to
make sure that I wasn't going to come up short on detail. Ronnie
had assured me that the area was a vibrant labyrinth of narrow
streets filled with bars and restaurants. But as I was beginning to
discover, like everywhere in Rome, Trastevere had its own rhythm
and the morning hours were slow and sleepy. The shutters were
down on the restaurants, the streets had the feel of the night after
a student party, the quiet of everyone crashed out on sofas waiting
to stagger into daylight for coffee and carbs. A few locals walked
their dogs and three-wheeler *api* – a sort of truck equivalent of a
Robin Reliant – took advantage of the lack of pedestrians to buzz
about unloading crates of lemons, tomatoes and garlic.

I walked on, relishing the freedom of not having a specific
destination. I stumbled across a mural on the wall of a hospital.
It was made up of eyes reflecting the Rome skyline in some of
the irises. I stood examining the details, revelling in both the
artistry and the fact that I had the luxury of time to stand and
stare – it seemed appropriate that I stopped to look, and the

object of my attention was eyes. I took a photo to send to
Maddie, hoping that cool street art might entice her here, even if
a mother who loved her a lot didn't.

Sitting on the kerb, I decided to see what I could find out
about the artist. He turned out to be from the UK, a man called
My Dog Sighs. I already loved him for his name, imagining him
at his easel with an ageing Labrador snuffling away on a duvet
in the corner of his studio. The mural, according to his website,
consisted of five hundred and forty eyes, with many containing
the silhouette of people who had a story connected to the hospital. Bravo, My Dog Sighs.

I opened Google Maps so I could remember the location if I
did manage to persuade Maddie to visit and, almost by reflex,
keyed in Giardino degli Aranci to see how far it was. A twenty-
minute walk. I sold it to myself as approaching it from a
different direction, exploring streets I hadn't yet walked, and
who knew what unlikely treasures I might come across?

I justified making the decision to go there by a need to apologise to Rico for my abrupt departure. I refused to think about
what I was expecting from seeing him again. However, the
possibility of having my ego soothed by an interesting and well-
travelled Italian was a definite draw. I could never explain that
to Maddie without copping a lecture about 'seeking validation
from a man'. She was strides ahead of me. At her age, I had one
eye on what everyone, not only men, thought of me – my hair-
cut, my clothes, even my laugh – torturing myself about stupid
things I said long after everyone was far more interested in
themselves. She'd turned out so sassy and self-confident that, if I
ever ventured an opinion that what she was wearing might give
the wrong impression, she would snap, 'What other people
think of me is their problem, not mine.' Which was a far cry
from worrying not only about what people thought of me, but of
Maddie as well. I also possessed a special ability to blush on

behalf of people I didn't even like when they made fools of themselves.

I turned in to the Giardino and my heart jumped when I saw Rico there. He raised a hand and burst into 'She', which immediately brought to mind an image of Joel watching *Notting Hill* with me. After having rolled his eyes all the way through, he'd finally had a tear at the happy ending. I hoped that his days in Paris were interspersed with memories so powerful it speared his soul to consider that we might not make any more. All that love we had couldn't just have disappeared.

I waved and went to sit on the wall overlooking the city, as self-conscious as a teenager. Rico put my colouring-up ability to the test straightaway. He boomed out, 'Could the woman with the sunglasses' – which, to be fair, didn't narrow it down much – unlike his next words – 'the blonde hair and the only one here crazy enough to wear a T-shirt in March come to the microphone please?'

I glanced round to see him beckoning to me. I smiled a no, but by then, a few people were craning in my direction.

'Resistance is *inutile*. I cannot sing another word until the lady sitting on the wall comes to tell me her choice of song.'

A group of Italians started gesturing. '*Vai! Vai!*'

I had no choice. I climbed down and headed over to Rico, to the sound of cheering. With all eyes upon me, the forty steps between us stretched for an eternity as I became acutely conscious of how I was walking. My mouth was fixed into what I hoped was a casual grin but in truth, probably looked like I'd taken a bite of something disgusting and was puzzling out how I could discreetly dispose of it.

He put up his hand, gesturing five minutes to everyone else and switched off his microphone. 'Such a pleasure to see you again. I thought you'd disappeared like Cenerentola.'

'Cenerentola?' I repeated, cursing the heat flooding my face.

'Cinderella.'

I searched my mind for some witty riposte but found them to be thin on the ground.

'So? What brings you here?' Rico asked.

I told a half-truth that I hadn't properly appreciated everything last time I came and wanted a second look.

'Including me?' The sheer confidence of the man, his eyes shining with such merriment, drew me into his banter.

'Maybe,' I said, the word tumbling out in a flippant and flirtatious way that took me by surprise.

'I have a three-hour slot here. I've only just started. Meet me in Trastevere for lunch at one-thirty. In front of Santa Maria della Basilicata.' I wasn't sure whether it was this Italian or Italians in general, but second-guessing didn't seem to occur to Rico.

'I'm not sure where that is,' I said, giving myself a moment to think.

He threw his hands up in mock despair. 'Come on. You're better than that. Google works in Rome too, you know. It's the biggest church in Trastevere.'

I couldn't think of an excuse. Or whether I even wanted an excuse.

'I'll show you the best place for *abbacchio* – baby lamb. Now I must play. What do you want to hear? Your favourite song?'

I blurted out the title that I'd played on a loop after Joel had left. 'James Morrison? "Wonderful World"?'

He rubbed at the stubble on his chin. 'Nice choice. You can tell me later why you don't find it a wonderful world right now.'

I moved away and sat down to listen, closing my eyes as I let the lyrics of love, loss and hope of reconciliation speak to me.

I glanced at Rico apologetically as my mobile rang. Maddie. I couldn't ignore it. That pull to connect with her, to put her first, to make sure she was all right, was as strong now as it was when I'd been able to fix any upset with a hug and a biscuit.

'Maddie!'

'Mum.' I knew from that one word something was wrong.

'Are you okay?' I asked, getting to my feet and distancing myself from Rico.

'It's Dad.'

'What? What's happened? Is he all right?' My brain immediately leapt to swanning about Rome while Joel had been pushed in front of a Parisian train.

Once I'd ascertained he was still alive, I concentrated on following the torrent of words about her deciding to go home to have a break from everyone at uni: 'I was a bit peopled out, so I hopped on a train on the spur of the moment. I got to King's Cross at about 10 p.m. and I was walking through St Pancras to get the train to Purley—'

'Why did you come home so late?' I asked. 'I don't like the thought of you being on trains on your own at that time of night.'

'Mum! That's not the point. I was desperate for the loo, so I sneaked into that hotel by the station and Dad was sitting in the bar there.'

I pressed the phone to my ear. 'Why was he back in England?'

'That's just it.' She paused. 'He was having a drink with this middle-aged woman.'

I frowned. 'Who was she?'

'Some woman called Nicky. One of Dad's colleagues. The thing is, they were embarrassed, like I'd caught them in the act of something.'

I was terrified to ask the question that would put an entirely different lens on everything I thought I knew. And certainly on everything I hoped for.

'What gave you that impression?' Even as my stomach took on that sick feeling of dread and fright, I stopped myself from interrogating her about whether they were kissing, holding hands, popping olives into each other's mouths.

Maddie rattled on, as though she wanted to deliver what she knew to me, so I could convert it into something unthreatening and trivial, something that didn't change our lives. 'He was awkward, talking about what a surprise it was to see me, and giving me some bullshit about having an unexpected meeting in London, just over for the day, and shooting off on Eurostar first thing in the morning.'

'It's probably true, love,' I said, trying to convince myself. 'He perhaps felt guilty for not telling you he was coming, not making a weekend of it so he could visit you.'

Maddie grunted. 'Do you think he's having an affair with her?' Her voice quivered and my decision to come to Rome had never seemed more ill-advised as my heart stretched across the miles. I longed to pull her to me and confirm everything would be okay. But even if I'd been standing next to her, I couldn't have offered that reassurance. I had no idea what was going on with Joel any more.

'Did you ask him?' I said.

I registered Rico singing the last lines of the song I'd requested and the distant clapping from the group of people at the viewing point. I turned my back on them all.

I strained to hear Maddie, who was really crying now. 'I sort of exploded. Started shouting about him being so selfish and you being selfish. No one stopping to consider for a minute what it's like for me, with no parents in the country and him bloody sniffing round another woman the minute you're out the way. He's always lying. First telling me that he had to go to Paris for work and then making out it was a temporary thing and that you just needed a bit of time apart. Have you being hiding things as well? Did you know he was seeing someone?'

I felt the sting of injustice. I was attempting, albeit in an unorthodox way, to save my marriage. There were so many elements to this, my brain felt hot trying to sift out the most important one. Still Maddie. Still her safety, her happiness.

'No! I don't think he's having an affair, love. You might have jumped to the wrong conclusion. Talk me through it.' I felt as though I was standing right next to an aircraft preparing to depart, the roaring in my head so loud I couldn't think, my questions rapid and disjointed. 'So what happened then? Where are you now? Is anyone with you?'

'I was going to go home, but instead Foz picked me up from Purley station. I stayed at his for the night and I'm on a train to Leeds now. My housemates are there.'

Foz. The dope-smoking friend from sixth form that I'd so strongly disapproved of had turned out to be the only port in Maddie's storm. I shouldn't have come here.

'Dad let you disappear off, without trying to stop you?' I didn't dare approach the whole other fury about his preferring to spend time with another woman rather than racing up the motorway to see his daughter and what the implications might be. It felt so much safer to focus on his shortcomings as a parent in that particular instant.

I was vaguely conscious of Rico bringing another song to a close as Maddie choked out her reply. 'Dad came running down the road after me, but I told him to get lost.'

I had the distinct feeling that Maddie was cleaning up her language in the relaying of the story.

'And did he "get lost"?'

'I've always been able to outrun him. Will you talk to Dad and find out what's going on?' Maddie asked. 'I mean, is this total BS that you're having a break and really you're getting a divorce and no one's bothered to tell me?'

'From my side, I definitely don't want a divorce. And Dad's always had a lot of female colleagues. But I will speak to him. I'll call you later,' I said, desperate for a bit of space to process what Maddie was telling me.

There was a pause. When she spoke again, her voice was soft and pleading. 'Can you come home?'

'Do you really want me to? You're not even living in Purley at the moment.'

'I'd feel better knowing you're there, though.'

The temptation to jump on a plane and rush to her was overwhelming. Every instinct in me was crying out to make her feel safe in the same way I'd been able to by stroking her hair when she'd had a nightmare as a little girl. But Maddie had her own life now. It was still term-time and even if I did a dramatic plane, train and automobile dash to England, it was entirely possible that Maddie would be too busy to come home and I'd spend my time twiddling my thumbs in Purley, waiting for a crumb of communication, let alone an eyes-on sighting of my only child.

'Let me make some phone calls and then we'll talk again.'

'Okay, Mum. Love you.'

I shoved my mobile into my handbag, walked towards Rico, mouthing, 'Sorry, I have to go. I can't have lunch.'

He put his thumb up in an 'Are you okay?' gesture.

I shook my head.

Goodness knows what I'd been thinking of. Pathetic me, assuming I could practise my flirting without it being any more complicated than that. That somehow I'd win my husband round with some spontaneity and a few well-timed 'amore mio'.

Rico waved a card in my direction, while still managing to sing the lovely lines of John Lennon's 'Imagine'. I took it just so I could escape and stuffed it into my pocket without looking at it. My maternal heart was aching with the desire to grab the first flight to London. I was primed to fix everything so Maddie could avoid being confronted by the brutal truth that her parents were flawed human beings whose marriage was currently held together by a diaphanous thread.

I walked down the hill, my brain picking through Maddie's

words. I wavered between believing that Joel was really over for a meeting with a colleague and asking myself why he hadn't rung Maddie to see if they could meet up. But maybe men, or more specifically, Joel, didn't have that invisible string, tugging him towards his child. I'd meet her for an hour if I had the chance, but I could easily imagine Joel compartmentalising work in London and his daughter two and a half hours' train journey away.

I headed towards the centre, distracted for a moment by a sign for the Bocca della Verità – the Mouth of Truth. I'd vaguely read something about it. Now would be a great time for a thunderbolt from above about what was truth and what was Maddie getting the wrong end of the stick. On impulse, I joined the short queue of people, lining up to place their hands in the mouth of a round stone face on the church wall. I stood behind two Americans who were laughing about the fact that legend had it that anyone telling a lie would have their fingers bitten off. 'So, Todd, you'd better not be having an affair.'

My heart ached with the nostalgia of being that wife who could joke, smug in the security of a rock-solid marriage. I offered to take a photo of them both and caught myself cynically capturing the image and thinking, *Give you something to look back on when it all goes belly up so you can remind yourself it wasn't all bad.*

I felt idiotic sticking my hand in the stone mouth without anyone to snap a photo. A German tourist offered to do it but I nearly refused out of embarrassment. Finally I accepted – if I ended up running back to England in the next day or two, it would be the only photo I had of myself in Rome.

I left the church and strode home, wrestling with what Maddie had told me. I passed the beggars on the corner of the Vatican, struck again by the disparity between the grand wealth of St Peter's mere metres away and the homelessness that was so evident, especially in the evenings. Rome was a city of such contradictions. A metaphor for life, really.

The initial numbness from the shock of Maddie's call was wearing off as the gates swung open. I wanted to sit on my terrace and mull over it all calmly and objectively. I needed to reach a conclusion that wasn't coloured by Maddie's outrage and my need to protect. My heart sank as I bumped into Ronnie, who was climbing onto her Vespa, and instructing Strega to sit on the footplate. Given my experience of the Rome traffic so far, she'd been lucky to make it to her seventies.

She rested her helmet on the handlebars. 'Hi! How are you getting on? Have you found many things of beauty?'

In that moment, I couldn't have cared less about the sunlight catching coloured glass in a convent window and frogs spouting water in fountains. I tried to satisfy her with a generic, 'Everywhere in Rome is beautiful! I've been spoilt for choice.'

She clapped her hands. 'Wonderful. This evening, you must come up and tell me everything. An aperitivo about six-thirty? We'll see if you're ready for your next challenge.'

I was all geared up to perform the following day and I was really not in the mood to wax lyrical about Rome when the rest of my life was going up in smoke. But Ronnie was a woman who managed to make invitations sound like three-line whips. Although it was fair enough to assume that I didn't have a queue of social engagements.

She jammed her helmet on her head without waiting for an answer. I'd have to develop a migraine. That didn't feel like too much of a stretch.

I walked into the apartment and onto the terrace. The nearby church bells were chiming and, a couple of rooftops away, I watched two workmen replacing the terracotta tiles, walking along the highest ridge with careless agility. Eventually, I dragged my gaze away. I couldn't ignore what Maddie had told me.

Before I lost my nerve, before I allowed myself to imagine what it would mean if Joel confirmed Maddie's suspicions as true, I dialled his number. I quickly tried to prepare a pithy message to leave if it went to voicemail. But Joel picked up. 'Beth! How are you?'

I'd intended to be calm, to winkle out the truth one way or the other. Instead, hearing him say my name so gently, as though he'd been holed up in a Paris mansard longing for my call, as though I was the one refusing to communicate, made all my fears explode into furious accusations. 'We're supposed to be doing our best to save our marriage. I'm in Rome, discovering who I am and, more importantly, who I could be, so we can have a future together that won't bore you rigid. You haven't even given me a chance. While I'm looking at my own behaviour and trying to change, you're rushing on to the next woman, seeing if there's something better out there. You've got to make an effort too. This can't all be on me or we might as well call it a day now.'

'Hey, hang on a minute, Maddie got completely the wrong end of the stick.' He explained how he'd come back to sort out a cock-up in the London office and he was tying up loose ends with his colleague Nicky, who'd really pulled her finger out to help him. 'Otherwise I'd have been stuck in England for the weekend and had to pick it up again on Monday.'

'You could have visited Maddie. Or even gone to the house to check it's still standing.'

'I thought the last thing she'd want is me turning up when she's planned a weekend clubbing with her mates.'

'Did you even ask her?'

Joel sighed. 'No. I didn't. I hold my hands up, I should have done. I was just focused on proving myself at work.'

Which was what I'd suspected. Despite my stern instructions to myself, relief fizzed in my heart. 'Why did you have to go for a drink with Nicky, though? Why not sort it all out at the office?'

'Bloody hell, Beth. We'd worked really hard. She was getting the tube to King's Cross and I fancied having a drink to celebrate resolving the issue. Hard as it might be for you to accept, I miss having someone ordinary to chat to. I'm either only half grasping the conversation because I'm at a work dinner and have to rely on all my French colleagues being polite enough to speak English, or I'm having room service on my own.'

Given that he'd chosen Paris over staying at home with his dull wife, it was tempting to tell him to stay on the line while I fetched my violin. Luckily, the mature version of me won the day. 'So you're definitely not having an affair then?' I was pretty sure he'd already ruled that out, but it was better to double-check now than have to text fifty follow-up questions later.

I could almost imagine Joel's mouth twist into one of his scornful expressions, the kind he used when I tried to explain anything political to Maddie.

'That'll be a no. Maddie came blundering in, decided what was going on, blew her stack, wouldn't listen to a word I said and disappeared.'

Ferocious mother love prevented me from being a total pushover. 'And you gave up looking for her? Knowing she was running around London in a state.'

'No. I'm not the hopeless father you make me out to be. I tracked her phone, saw she'd got on a train and then I realised she was at Foz's. You know what she's like. You can't reason with her when she's in one of her funks.'

I had to concede that Maddie was a hothead and there was no talking to her until the thermometer moved downwards.

'She's asking me to return to England,' I said, hating myself for still needing Joel's approval, Joel's permission for anything.

'That's up to you.' His voice was resigned, as though he'd

expected me to give up on Rome and scuttle off to the comfort blanket of home as soon as I could.

'I don't really want to,' I said, the determination in my voice surprising me. 'I'm worried about her, though, Joel.'

'I know that, but Maddie's an adult. She's got her own life. She's in Leeds most of the time. We both left home at eighteen and never went back,' he said, as though there was a one size fits all for flying the nest and whatever he did would be the perfect mould for his daughter too.

'She has had a bit of a shock with us splitting up.' I was testing the water to see if Joel was going to give me a clue as to which way the tide was turning.

'We haven't made any definite decisions about that yet, have we?' He paused. 'I can't pretend I'm not jealous of you out there with all those Italian blokes.'

That was a turn-up for the books. Jealousy wasn't an emotion I associated with Joel. I was hopeless at playing the game, though, and immediately countered with, 'Well, I'm not out having dinner or drinks with any men.' I decided to discount the lunch with Rico. That was daytime safe.

'This time apart is about both of us living the best lives we can and finding out whether ultimately we want to be together. But hats off to you that you've been brave enough to go to Italy.' The 'I didn't think you had it in you' reverberated into the silence.

I registered a surge of satisfaction that this off-the-wall idea hadn't been for nothing. That at the very least, I'd earned a bit of admiration and recognition from Joel.

Nonetheless, I still wanted to beg, to tell him that I'd forget Rome, that I'd come out to Paris, that I would do *whatever it took*. But Joel suddenly turned all formal, as though he'd said too much, 'Right, well, good to catch up with you. Let me chat to Maddie and smooth things over with her. I'll keep you posted. I'll make sure she's okay – she can come out to Paris for some of the Easter holiday.'

He rang off, managing to leave me more confused than reassured. I resigned myself to going to Ronnie's that evening. I had to distract myself or go mad wondering.

I headed to the shops. At the very least, I should take Ronnie a bottle of wine. I followed Google to a Carrefour supermarket and took a basket at the door. Foreign supermarkets had always intrigued me, as though looking at the produce offered up an insight into the priorities of the nation. I lingered over the focaccia, the olive loaves, the folded pizzas. Joel was a sucker for posh bread...

How did people do it? How did they unpick that thought process that always defaulted to the enmeshed consideration of their spouse's likes and dislikes? I forced myself to buy a ciabatta stuffed with nuts, which he hated. Wine for Ronnie posed another challenge. I drank New Zealand Sauvignon, so I didn't know anything about Italian wines. I was so terrified of turning up with a bottle of the most laughable plonk that I plucked up the courage to ask a man choosing his wines for a *'buon vino italiano'*. He was only too delighted to be of assistance, insisting that I tried *'un buon Cesanese'*, which, with lots of gesturing, I understood was made from a variety of grape from Lazio, the area around Rome.

I approached the checkout feeling as though I was nearly a native with the inside track on local wine. Until the assistant pointed at my nut ciabatta and demanded to know where the price ticket was. 'You weigh,' she instructed before waving me towards the bread counter. I scarpered off and stood looking at the bewildering array of bakery labels on the scales. I clearly dithered for far too long because she swooped round the corner, snatched the bag from me, stabbed at the right button and said, 'Next time, this one!'

I shot after her as she returned to the checkout. To my

horror, she hadn't continued to serve the person behind me. Instead, there was a queue of fifteen people snaking around the little supermarket with disgruntled faces that were not the slightest bit pacified by my 'Scusi, scusi.'

Trudging up the hill with my purchases, I wished that I could get the simplest of things right. I'd been deranged to think moving abroad, even to a city as beautiful as Rome, would solve anything. By the time I knocked on Ronnie's door, I'd decided. The answer to saving my marriage wasn't some stupid rebellion in Italy. At the very least, I needed to be at home for Maddie, to help her make sense of what was happening to our family.

Ronnie flung the door open. 'Marina's joining us.' She said it as though that was some kind of pay-day bonus rather than another bossy person I'd have to find the oomph to stand up to. Ronnie waved her hand in a 'What can you do?' sort of way. 'Apparently, Marina has a "suitor" taking her for dinner tomorrow night, so if it's okay with you, you can tell us everything you've discovered about Rome this evening instead.'

I sighed to myself. At least I'd get it all over in one go. 'I'm happy to do whatever suits you both, thank you.' I handed her the bottle.

'Oooh someone's cottoned onto the best vintages, thank you.'

With a stupid amount of pride, I told her about my wine hero in the supermarket.

'Brilliant. You'll be a local before you know it.'

I managed a smile. I wasn't sure what the etiquette was for calling a halt to this experiment, given that it had been such a generous offer to a stranger in the first place. I didn't want to seem ungrateful. Marina was there to fill any second of silence when I might have been able to think. She stood up on the terrace, handed me a dark-coloured drink and offered me some mushroom crostini. 'Ciao, bellissima. A negroni sbagliato for you – vermouth, Campari and Prosecco.'

'Thank you,' I said, sipping the cocktail and feeling an immediate hit of alcohol. If they had aperitivi like this every evening, they must have livers like pickled walnuts.

Marina slugged hers down. 'Rome is suiting you, Beth. You've caught a bit of colour. I hope you've been wearing sunscreen.'

I nodded, tempted to say that I already had a mum back home, and strangely enough, at age fifty, I didn't need Marina in loco parentis.

'That's rich coming from you, Marina,' Ronnie said. 'You used to lie on a beach with foil under your chin to reflect the sun onto your face.'

Marina frowned as Ronnie spoilt her sanctimony in the way old friends with long memories do.

'I have an Italian complexion, not your and Beth's English rose skin.'

Ronnie waved a hand at her. 'Anyway, sshh. I want to hear what beautiful things have brought joy to Beth's heart this week.'

It was like a viva for an exam for which I wasn't entirely sure of the syllabus. I got a hit in early with the off-the-tourist-trail Coppedè area. They both murmured their approval and I felt the victory of surpassing their expectations.

'Surely you didn't walk all the way out there?' Ronnie asked.

'No, I took the tram, but walked back.'

My transport arrangements appeared to be of limited interest to Marina, who peered at me so intensely I fought the urge to wipe my mouth in case I had something stuck to it. She relaxed back into her chair. 'You're looking well. You've got a very nice décolletage. You should make more of it. You really need to cut your hair, though.'

The way Marina piped up with such personal comments left me slightly winded. I wondered if it was a two-way thing, whether she would take it in her stride if I suddenly announced that she should stop dyeing her hair jet black 'at her age' and go for something a bit softer to make her skin look less sallow. I pretended to myself I'd try it out. For now, I didn't want to encourage further scrutiny so I started to flick through the photos of the various treasures that had caught my eye this week.

Ronnie leaned in to look. 'Love that door knocker. Fabulous archway with the graffiti. Is that in Via del Pellegrino?'

How I wanted to be that person who said, 'No, actually, it's just off—' but I muttered about it being not far from Piazza Navona, limited as I was in geographical terms by bridges, proximity to St Peter's and the main squares.

Ronnie took the mobile from me for a closer inspection, then carried on swiping. I remembered too late that I'd taken some pictures of Rico. She thrust the phone towards Marina. 'Now, look at that thing of beauty. He's singing straight to you there.'

Marina deemed Rico worthy of getting her glasses out of her bag. She peered at my phone and I waited for her cutting comment. Instead, she stuck out her bottom lip in approval. '*Proprio bello.* I bet he takes your mind off that stupid husband of yours.'

All the little humiliations of my day gathered in the pause as I took a gulp of my drink. I didn't have to put up with these two women tearing chunks out of my self-esteem, which, let's face it, didn't have many chunks to spare. I had to call time on this misguided undertaking.

I turned away from Marina and addressed Ronnie. 'Actually, Ronnie, I spoke to my daughter and to Joel today and decided that I should return to England. I'm sorry to let you down, but my daughter is very upset about the whole situation and needs me at home. I don't think Joel and I can work anything out while I'm here and he's in Paris.'

Out of the corner of my eye, Marina was wagging her finger. The temptation to lean over, snap it off and fling it into the sitting room for Strega to chew on was real.

Ronnie pursed her lips in a disappointed way. 'I understand that mother's reaction.'

I was sure Marina was pulling a face in the periphery of my vision, but I wasn't going to allow her the microphone.

Ronnie uncorked the wine while I braced myself for a left-of-field blow.

'But Maddie is living her own life, no? Not at home? So, are you going to move to her university town?'

'No, no, I wouldn't do that.'

'So, let's say you give up this challenge and you go back to England because she's asked you to. How often does she come home of her own accord?' Ronnie finished off her cocktail and poured herself a generous measure of wine.

I blustered about her staying in Leeds for the whole of the first term because she was scared to miss out and how she'd jumped at the chance to spend Christmas at the ski lodge. I omitted the bit about when I'd gone to visit in November and stayed for a couple of nights. I'd ended up sitting in my hotel room watching Netflix after she had rushed dinner with me so she could catch up with friends who were going clubbing.

'So apart from the occasional moment when she'd like you to be on tap because she has a moment of downtime, she's making the most of every opportunity that comes her way without much thought for whether you're on your own or not?'

I put my glass on the table, gazing for a second at the vines painted on the ceramic top. I tried not to sound too defensive when I spoke, but I wasn't having Ronnie thinking badly of Maddie. 'She's not a selfish girl. I'm glad she's making friends and expanding her horizons. I can always return to Rome another year, though obviously it won't be quite like this experience.'

Marina was unusually silent. But Ronnie had plenty to say. 'I don't think your daughter is any different from anyone else her age. All young people are selfish. It's how they survive and separate from us. She will feel guilty and obliged to visit if you give in to her desire to have you back in the family home at the precise moment she should be flying free.'

Ronnie's statement had a sweeping criticism about it, but I also recognised the truth that any maternal clinging from me would meet with a robust pair of secateurs. I'd been the same at Maddie's age, old enough to understand that – theoretically – my parents had thoughts and feelings but not yet considerate enough to override what I wanted to do and adjust my behaviour to avoid hurting them.

Ronnie held her hand up, a big sapphire glinting in the sunlight. The empress of the house had more wisdom to impart. As unpalatable as her observations were, I couldn't deny that she had tapped into the reservations I had about whether Maddie would really spend any more time with me than she did now. And if our interactions were over FaceTime, did it matter whether I was in a cul-de-sac in Purley or a sunny kitchen in Rome?

'Secondly, is running home the moment she asks the best thing you can teach her? That it doesn't matter what you're doing, what adventures you are discovering, a woman's role is to dance to everyone else's tune, always putting themselves last? Which, I'm sorry to say, is what brought you here in the first place. From what I understand, you bore the main domestic responsibility while Maddie was growing up and Joel thanked you for it by disappearing off to Paris and telling you how tedious you'd become.'

Ronnie and Marina were a world-class double act in not dressing up the truth. I'd long ago recognised the veracity of what Ronnie said, but her words still provoked the fresh burn of first-blow acceptance. The basis of her logic was sound, though, and I couldn't summon up any kind of plausible counter-argument.

Marina's silence had obviously led to too much air storing up in her lungs that she needed to expel. 'I don't have kids, so I can't say, but I've had three husbands. None of them decided to love me more because I returned when they'd behaved appallingly. I learnt my lesson with the third one.'

'Where is he now?' I asked, hoping my desire to know many, many more details wasn't too obvious.

'He died waiting for me to make up my mind about whether to forgive him for gambling away our farmhouse in Puglia. The delay paid off in the end. Instead of getting half of what he owned, I got all of it.' She stroked her necklace. 'Now I'm taking the view that diamonds are a girl's best friend. No more men for me.'

From the way Ronnie raised her eyebrows, I wasn't sure that the whole truth and nothing but the truth was unfolding before me.

I had to hand it to Marina. She was very different from the women in their seventies I came across when I picked my mother up from her bridge club.

Marina tapped my phone screen and pointed to Rico. 'Personally, I'd take a little breather from a difficult marriage with this chap. You might find that what you think you want is not what you actually want. And if you do make up with Joel and have to stand being married to the same person for the next thirty years, you'll have had an exciting interlude in the meantime.'

I was so flabbergasted to be receiving relationship advice that amounted more or less to 'stop being so square and go and get laid' from someone knocking eighty that I laughed. I wasn't going to have a fling with anyone, let alone a man who'd led such an exciting, carefree life that if Joel found me boring, I'd keel over with the pressure of being entertaining enough for him.

Marina launched in again. 'It's not selfish to pursue your own dreams. I think it's good for people to learn that they can't take you for granted. Give them space to miss you. I bet they'll both appreciate you more when you go back.' She winked. 'If you go back.'

I pressed my fingers into the cool of the table, assessing whether she was right or not.

Ronnie put her hand over mine. 'You talk as though it's a given that you have plenty of time for other escapades. But what if this is the last one? Would you still be glad to have given up this chance to do your own thing for a few months? I'm a big fan of the "If not now, when?" philosophy.'

And more than any other argument, that splinter of persuasion dug deep, reminding me of my dad. He'd postponed his lifelong dream to have a month in Australia and snorkel on the Great Barrier Reef until my parents retired because Mum didn't want to use all her holiday entitlement in one go – 'I have to save a few days to take off before Christmas to get everything right.' However, when they'd eventually finished working, the years of smoking had caught up with him and he could barely walk upstairs, let alone snorkel with the stingrays. 'Don't wait to be happy, love,' was the last thing he ever said to me.

7

I'd intended to search for flights home, but Ronnie's words had unlocked something in me that I couldn't shake off. Everyone else was doing what they wanted. Was it so unreasonable to carve out a slot for myself? I'd be home again in fifty-nine days. Even Joel thought I should stick to my guns, though his opinion shouldn't carry any weight. Judging by Maddie's Instagram showing her with a group of friends wearing huge bunny ears and downing cocktails, she wasn't sitting at home waiting for my arrival.

Even Helen was too busy to FaceTime me, which felt like a far cry from her 'We can speak every day' assurances when she was encouraging me to come. Instead I'd had a series of short audio messages saying she couldn't wait to catch up with me, while never being free to do the actual catching up. She did, however, find time to send me passé cartoons about how men needed a medal for emptying the dishwasher. I guessed it was an attempt to make me feel better about a possible future where I'd never have to hunt for a lemon juicer put in the wrong place again. On the other hand, I couldn't fault how much she'd supported me in making a change when I needed to force Joel to sit up and take notice. Whereas some of my other friends had been openly scornful of my decision to leave for Italy – 'All your problems will still be here when you come back' – or worse, they'd already drifted away and pulled up the drawbridge as though a single woman in their midst would be gobbling up husbands like a frenzied shark.

I made peace with my indecision by electing to stay another week, if only to avoid allowing anyone the satisfaction of saying, 'See, you can't run away from yourself.' Which meant I'd have to tackle the task Ronnie had outlined the previous evening – 'if you find the courage to stay'. Those words alone sparked the desire in me to prove that I wasn't as cowardly as they assumed. The challenge she'd mentioned hadn't sounded too onerous: 'You need to rediscover the pleasure of food. There was a reason I asked you to write down what you eat in a typical week.'

I'd got in quickly with my defence. 'I haven't really both-ered much about cooking since I've been on my own.' I didn't add that most evenings since Maddie and Joel had left I had cheese on toast or a bowl of muesli for dinner, because, despite my best intentions, I simply couldn't bring myself to start chop-ping and peeling just for myself.

Marina hadn't been able to resist chipping in. 'Food is all part of living sensually. If your taste buds are alive, then the rest of you will be more vibrant too. Scotch eggs and cheese and onion quiche have no place in passion.'

I was grateful that she hadn't witnessed me scoffing Nutella out of the jar in an 'I need a quick feel-good fix' way, rather than a sensuous licking of the spoon as a come-on to Joel. No doubt Marina could have carried that off with aplomb. I was pretty sure that given the right circumstances Marina, chocolate spread and strategically placed strawberries would be natural bedfellows.

Ronnie had nodded her agreement. 'Go and reacquaint

yourself with the pleasure of choosing ingredients and cooking them from scratch.'

'I'm not a particularly good cook,' I'd remarked.

Ronnie had smiled. 'I thought that when I first came to Italy. I could just about cook potatoes, pork chops and boiled carrots. But cooking is about trusting that you can tell when something needs more salt, a squeeze of lemon, a dash of vinegar.'

'But what if you don't have that confidence?' Cooking Sunday lunch for more than the three of us made me flustered and bad-tempered.

'You will acquire it.' She had passed me a piece of paper. 'So, let's consider my original premise. The big things are the little things. A simple pasta with tomato and basil sauce – it's incredible how good that can be. And pesto. But not the horrible pesto you buy in jars in England. Homemade pesto. Where you can taste the punch of the freshly picked basil. Of course, it's not typical of Rome, more a dish from Liguria, but it is the perfect start to illustrate the difference between fresh and manufactured. And, next Saturday, you can cook for us. A whole week to practise.'

I had glanced down at the recipes. On the face of it, they looked simple enough with only a few ingredients.

Marina had leaned forward. 'I know you are going to say you're not sure whether you will still be here, but you will be. You're a woman with courage.' She'd raised her glass. 'To Beth and all the dormant passions within her.'

I should have hated everything about her, but she was oddly, maddeningly, contradictorily likeable.

Ronnie had waved me out. 'Don't leave. We'll be expecting two plates of perfectly prepared pasta next Saturday. Tell Beppe on the market stall that "Ronica" sent you.'

So instead of packing my things and making peace with my failed experiment, the next morning, I headed off to the market round the corner clutching my list of ingredients. I wandered about, avoiding making eye contact, wondering which of the stallholders was Beppe. I sat on a bench, watching how the stall-holders interacted, bringing each other coffee, offering little tastes of produce from their stalls – cheese, olives, salami, even a spoonful of neat olive oil. It seemed to lead to lots of gesturing and throwing up of hands as though they'd been on a lifetime quest for the perfect parmesan or prosciutto and the universe had finally delivered it.

Eventually, I heard a woman in a van piled high with wheels of cheese shout over to a weather-worn man in a dark blue linen shirt. He'd been like a busy ant all morning, lifting up bunches of grapes for approval and sniffing each melon before selecting the one that met his criteria. 'Beppe! Beppe!' She indicated a wizened old lady, bent over and struggling to pull her trolley.

Beppe ran over, helped her to my bench and asked her what she needed. He returned to his stall, and began putting things in paper bags. Onions. Tomatoes. Courgettes. Lemons. Turning each one over, squeezing it, discarding it, picking up another. Despite a queue forming, he came back to the woman and took time showing her what he'd chosen. She tested the ripeness with her bony fingers and nodded as Beppe packed it all care-fully into her trolley bag. It was hard not to compare him with the guy on my local market stall at home, who growled if you so much as looked like you were going to have a sneaky feel of an avocado in an effort to avoid either a bullet or rotten brown sludge. I loved Beppe for his compassion, for not growing impa-tient with the woman. I also totally admired her dedication to ensuring she wasn't being fobbed off with the squashed toma-toes from the bottom of the box despite looking as though the effort of opening her fridge might be an ordeal.

I stayed sitting while the queue at Beppe's stall dissipated, then ambled over, hoping his patience with the elderly lady would extend to the foreigner stuttering through her vegetable vocabulary.

He smiled. '*Signora*?'

I panicked, despite practising the words before I left home. 'Do you speak English?'

'A little. What do you like?'

I showed him the list. 'Ronica sent me,' I said, hoping that would act as a catalyst for tolerance and an excuse for being such a linguistic dunce.

'You're family?'

'No, no. A friend.'

He put a large vine of tomatoes into the scales. That tantalising scent of fresh tomatoes wafted over to me, making me realise I hadn't smelt it in years, not since my dad grew them on his allotment. I pushed down the familiar feelings of loss. I didn't have room today for the grief that I'd become accustomed to, that always accompanied me quietly. Not when I had the hot-off-the-press hurt of Joel's behaviour raging away.

'It's a shame that the daughter don't never visit. I have three daughters and they are always coming. Papa, we need a ladder. Papa, bring some olive oil. The youngest one was in school with Nadia. I know them all, her husband, Matteo, too.'

Beppe sneered openly as he said Matteo's name. From the little I'd gathered from Marina's asides, there was a definite story about that marriage. I couldn't help being curious to know more. I thought Beppe muttered the word '*bastardo*', but I couldn't be sure and I was at a loss as to how to tease more details out of him without coming across as a nosey foreigner.

Beppe became preoccupied with darting backwards and forwards to his van, searching for a bigger, better bunch of basil when, as far as I could see, the huge sheaves already on display were far superior to the five anaemic strands that I bought in the supermarket at home. He packed a head of garlic the size of a fist into the bag and laid the herbs gently on top.

'So, don't cut the basil. You must do like this,' he said, ripping a leaf. Suddenly, he looked up. 'I don't see Ronica in lots of time. How long you stay with her?'

'About two months more.' As I said it – a bit like flipping a coin and knowing which outcome would be disappointing – I felt the calm of reaching the right decision.

As I passed over my euros, Beppe said, 'I see you again.' He stuffed a big fan of rocket into my bag. 'This for Ronica. She always say that Italian rucola is best in the world.'

Buoyed by Beppe's friendliness, I dared to ask the woman in the van for 'parmigiano'. She didn't laugh at my accent and offered me little chunks to taste, which made me resolve never to buy a ready-grated bag or anything that was sold in a plastic triangle ever again. In fact, right now, it was almost impossible to imagine that I could ever go back to snatching up a super-market egg and cress sandwich with a sell-by date three days in the future. I even allowed myself a daydream about opening an Italian deli, peering at my customers through prosciutto hanging from the ceiling, waxing lyrical about the olives from Sicily and the dried tomatoes from Sardinia. For a second, with the same ephemeral beauty of an oriental poppy on a windy day, I had a fleeting glimpse of the possibilities of a whole new future... Which I immediately dismissed, reminding myself that I already had the life I wanted, I just needed to get Joel on board.

Nevertheless, I returned to the apartment triumphant, forgetting for an instant that I still had to transform these deli-cious ingredients into a dinner that Ronnie and Marina would find acceptable, though I'd had the foresight to buy double so I could practise.

From Ronnie's open window, I heard her voice, raised. 'Nadia. Of course you will always have a home here. But I cannot throw her out on the street.'

The gates clanked behind me.

'The other two apartments are full of junk, the kitchen is

missing in one and the bathroom is broken in the other. ... It's not up to you who I invite to live in that apartment. Your father left it to me, not to you.' Her voice was rising with frustration.

I realised with a jolt that the row was about me living there. I shouldn't be eavesdropping, but I couldn't tear myself away. I heard a chair scrape along the floor and her footsteps on the terracotta tiles. It must be hell to live underneath a large family in these buildings.

I paused at the entrance to the palazzo, my ears straining. Ronnie's voice drifted in and out.

'No. I am perfectly capable of sorting it out. What's the earliest you want to come? Mid-April? No. Not possible. She's leaving in mid-May. I can't throw her out. Of course I can't.'

What did that mean? It would be sod's utter law that having decided to stay, my host was going to evict me. Not truly appreciating things until they were snatched away from me was becoming a bit of a pattern.

There was a noise on the terrace and I shoved my key into the front door.

In the days that followed, I dreaded a knock at the door and an apologetic Ronnie explaining that she was so sorry but that she had to ask me to leave. I didn't see her to talk to, occasionally crossing paths as she zipped off on her Vespa, Strega perching precariously. Having wavered and whinged about whether to stay, I couldn't blame Ronnie if she decided to take the path of least resistance and boot me out to placate her daughter. From what I'd gleaned so far, their relationship was pretty fraught without my presence complicating things further.

A friendly but perfunctory WhatsApp informed me that I should expect Marina and Ronnie at 7.30 p.m. on Saturday evening. I hadn't anticipated that they would come to me, which sent me into a flurry of panic about making sure the apartment was perfectly clean.

I was more nervous than I had been for my finals when Saturday morning rolled around. Instead of dipping a spoon into the pesto for the umpteenth time, asking myself whether it needed a fraction more salt or garlic, I decided to go and buy some flowers to make the terrace as beautiful as possible, so that even if my food was a disaster, they'd know that I'd tried.

Despite Marina's various 'suggestions' I'd yet to nail a wardrobe that was suitably elegant by Roman standards but could cope with the March sunshine. Clearly the Italian women my age, with their fur coats and puffa jackets in twenty-two degrees of heat, were on a superior form of HRT, because the mere sight of them made me burst into a hot sweat.

Today was not a day for getting any hotter and more bothered than necessary, so I opted for public transport, which I'd avoided since the ticket debacle on the tram. I nearly hopped off when the machine at the rear of the bus wasn't working, but the woman next to me uttered some kind of disapproving comment and snatched the ticket out of my hand to try herself. Finally satisfied that the issue was a technical one, not an incompetent foreigner one, she barked an instruction at the man next to her, which, to my ear, didn't seem to contain a 'please' or a 'do you mind'.

As if by magic, the ticket passed from person to person along to the machine at the front, with my heart thumping every time we stopped in case the inspectors got on, before finally making its way back to me. I thanked my saviour, but she wasn't on the cosy side of tourist helping. Instead, she gestured crossly and then launched into a marvellously angry rant, which if I was picking out the words correctly, not only encompassed the government and the council, but the Madonna herself. By the time I reached my stop to pick up flowers at the appropriately named Campo de' Fiori, I was quite exhausted by the level of emotion a ticket machine could engender. I'd love to let her loose on Joel.

I stood gawking at the flower stall with the buckets of blooms, wondering what would be considered classy. The hanging baskets of petunias? Sunflowers? Pots of hyacinths?

The stall owner threw his arms open. '*Signora?*' He presented me with so many options that I ended up with an armful of white roses and some lilies that I was less sure about because in my mind they were funeral flowers. However, he assured me that they would be a great hit. Again, like Beppe, he took great care selecting the perfect stems for me.

Emboldened by my floral success, I took a seat on one of the sunny café terraces and watched as people milled about the market, choosing plants, chatting to the traders who worked on the fruit and vegetable stalls, buying beakers of freshly squeezed pomegranate juice. England suddenly seemed a long way away, both in distance and emotion, as though I'd climbed out of my life into a different scrapbook of experiences, all together brighter and more energetic, as well as noisier.

I wasn't sure how long I sat there, marvelling at the importance of food and how much discussion it provoked. I'd never toss the plastic tray that billed itself as the 'Italian cold meat platter' into my trolley again without thinking of the blokes who worked on the deli counters here. They sold salami with the same seriousness and attention to detail that an average Brit would expend choosing a nursing home for an ailing relative. Except as far as I could see, even in a city as big as Rome, the elderly didn't appear ignored and invisible. I wondered if Italy had a Minister for Loneliness like the UK.

After I'd finished my coffee, I headed over myself and bought some pecorino cheese and some *mortadella di amatrice* – a type of salami from Lazio – after turning down the fatty *guanciale* that the stallholder thought he was promoting by telling me it was made from the fat of pig cheeks. In my mind's eye, I could picture Maddie making gagging noises and declaring herself a vegan from hereon in.

I walked home, still pondering about how the older generation seemed so much more included in society here. The prospect of living on my own in old age if Joel didn't come back dragged down my mood. I had a vision of eking out my years eating tinned soup with an expiry date ten years hence and fetching slices of bread from the freezer because a loaf would go mouldy before I could eat it. Maybe I'd move to Italy, where I could spend my days eating focaccia and prosciutto on park benches, nattering to all the other oldies in the square and talking to other people's children without their mothers jumping to the conclusion that I was a child snatcher.

The realisation that the afternoon had run away with me, and that in a mere three hours' time, Ronnie and Marina would be arriving to judge my culinary skill brought me out of my melancholy. I said aloud, 'I'm not going to think about sad things today.'

Back at the apartment, I put the flowers in vases, dotted them around the terrace and made sure that I didn't commit my usual faux pas of forgetting to fill up the ice trays. FaceTime sang into life on my phone just as I put down the last napkin. It was Helen, stuttering into view on the apartment's dodgy Wi-Fi.

She did the 'Hellloooo! Finally!' as though she'd tried to contact me hundreds of times. I was surprised at how annoyed I felt with her. I'd had visions of sharing my mini-adventures on a regular basis and had been looking forward to her being both envious and congratulatory that I'd been courageous enough to do this.

She gave me the rundown on work, her kids, the rain. Then she took her computer over to the mantelpiece in her lounge to show me the anniversary card her husband, Alan, had sent, along with a bouquet of roses. 'Bless him. Silver wedding anniversary next year! Maybe he'll take me to Rome and you can recommend lots of lovely places.'

'Congratulations.' I forced myself to be glad for her. I did allow through the churlish thought that I wouldn't want to be married for twenty-five years to a man who always looked permanently affronted, as though someone who hadn't paid for speedy boarding had jumped the queue when the flight was called.

I found myself telling her about Joel and how Maddie had lost the plot when she'd come across him having a drink with another woman.

Helen sniffed. 'I'm not sure buying someone of the opposite sex a quick beer after work means he's playing the field. Maddie's always been a bit dramatic about everything, hasn't she?'

I leapt to Maddie's defence. 'She's had a lot of change to deal with. I don't think there's ever a good age for your parents to split up.'

'Plenty of kids survive it, though. It's not the end of the world, is it?'

I should have dropped Maddie as a topic, but instead blurted out that she had put pressure on me to come home.

'That's beyond selfish. I hope you're not going to give in to that. She should be pleased for you.'

There was something in Helen's tone, a casual criticism that was skating her to places she wouldn't need an ice pick to fall through. Childishly, I wanted to start ranting about how rude and selfish her own kids were on the one occasion I'd been to her house for a barbecue. They'd never looked up from their phones to say hello, then had fallen on the chocolates I'd brought like they'd never had a hazelnut swirl in their lives.

'Is it that unusual to want one of us in England? It's not as though she can rely on Joel to come running.'

Helen adopted a more conciliatory tone. 'Oh yes, I know. Poor girl. She's still young. She probably feels quite alone.'

I didn't want her speaking about Maddie as though she was an abandoned puppy. She couldn't win.

I changed the subject. 'Anyway, when I spoke to Joel the other day, he said he was jealous of all the Italian men I was meeting, so maybe our plan is working.'

'Did he? And are you meeting lots of lovely Italian men?'

I couldn't decide whether she sounded envious that I had the freedom to flirt, or incredulous, as though I was so past it, no suave Italian in his right mind would give me a second glance. 'Not really. I mean, they're generally more flirtatious than British men, but I wouldn't know how to give someone the come-on now if my life depended on it. I have had a bit more male attention than usual, I suppose.' I ground to a halt, still irritated with her comments about Maddie. I didn't feel in the mood for telling her about Rico. I eyed the clock over the doorway to the kitchen. 'I'm going to have to go. I've got a cookery challenge tonight.'

'You? Hope they eat before they come!' Helen sipped her coffee, the mug shaking as she giggled.

I was the first to admit cooking wasn't my specialist subject, but Helen's idea of gourmet was serving cashews instead of peanuts. Her attitude made me feel as though she preferred it when I was a snivelling wreck flailing about in failure rather than applauding me for succeeding on the adventure she'd encouraged me to undertake. I clicked off the call, brooding about how yet another person hadn't met my expectations.

By the time Marina and Ronnie knocked on the door, I was as jittery as if Charles and Camilla were my guests. Marina barrelled in first, marching out to the terrace with the confidence of someone who knew there was only one opinion in the room that counted. In her eyes anyway. She threw up her hands with delight. 'This looks beautiful.' She turned to Ronnie. 'See. Beth has taken to Italian aesthetics like a duck to water.'

I wanted to point out that I had bought and arranged flowers in my own house before. That I wasn't quite the polyester pinafore woman who had magically discovered a bit of style in Rome that she was making me out to be. When I searched my memory, though, I had to admit it was ages since I'd treated myself to flowers. And probably even longer since Joel had bought me any.

I'd tried to reach a compromise between being able to sit outside and not polluting the environment by keeping the gas heater on a low setting, but without asking, Marina whacked the heat up so high, I thought my eyebrows might singe off. They sat down, and once again, I found myself drawn to Ronnie. Unlike Marina, whose thoughts tended to canter out of her mouth like a horse spooked by a firework, Ronnie had a quiet authority. I craved her approval, for all the world a middle-aged pupil simultaneously hoping and dreading that her essay would be read out to the class.

I'd always been under the impression that Italian women didn't drink much, but Marina was glugging away and I topped up her glass for the second time. I blushed as she mindread my thoughts. 'My grandparents owned a hotel in Ireland. My mother always said any man that gets drunk is not a man, so my father practised long and hard so he could hold his drink.' I could quite see where Marina's contrary nature originated.

While Marina and Ronnie oohed and aahed over the platter of salami and cheese, I got up to put the pasta on. Ronnie came through. 'I'm saving you from Marina. You need a big pan of boiling water. No, not that one. Bigger. Salt. And take it off the heat one and a half minutes before you normally would. British people always overcook pasta. Marina will never let you forget it if you serve it *scotta*.'

Finally, I brought out a large bowl of pasta *al pesto*, and one with *pomodoro e basilico*, stressing about whether they were al dente enough. Goodness knows what the *MasterChef* contestants felt like when they served up their endeavours for a table of Michelin-starred chefs. Though I was reasonably sure that Marina's acerbic observations would be able to give any one of them a run for their money.

Ronnie and Marina twirled the spaghetti onto their forks. Marina chewed, her eyes narrowed as though she was in conversation with her taste buds. 'Well. Not bad. More salt. You British never put enough salt in anything.'

The Italians' attitude to salt contradicted their over-the-top health concerns about catching a cold if they were caught in a spring shower. On the couple of occasions there'd been a sudden downpour, their desire for shelter bordered on the hysterical.

Ronnie clapped her hands. 'Delicious. Well done.'

And for the first time – either because of the wine or because after talking to Helen, I couldn't be bothered to examine my feelings – I relaxed, the alcohol gliding around my body, my eyes flicking to the rooftops and all the lights glittering across Rome. I was here. In this magical city. I had a fleeting moment of gratitude that circumstances had forced me so far beyond my comfort zone.

Ronnie paid me the highest compliment by mopping up the pesto with a piece of bread, then taking a bit more of the tomato pasta, saying, 'Thank goodness Nadia isn't here to give me a lecture on overdosing on carbs.'

Marina leaned back in her chair. I readied myself for a curveball, some sartorial or social faux pas I was about to be made aware of. 'You know Ronnie's daughter is threatening to come and evict you?'

I looked at Ronnie, who, despite switching to Italian – rude!

– left me in no doubt that she was properly annoyed with Marina. Who obviously couldn't have cared less.

'I think we should evict Marina instead for shit-stirring,' Ronnie said. And rather than sticking to the topic I wanted to explore – whether I was about to be out on my ear – the two of them launched into who would employ the best solicitor and win the day.

I put my glass down, my sense of wellbeing immediately leaping to the familiar discomfort of tense anxiety. 'Do you want me to leave?'

Ronnie ran her fingers through her hair, making the blue tips stand on end. 'If I am to take on my daughter's wrath – and she is formidable – I need to know that you are in this for the long term? That all this dithering about going back is over?'

'This dithering about' as Ronnie described it felt unjust. I was only trying to protect my daughter and save my marriage to boot.

'It's probably best if I leave then. I didn't realise that there was a conflict of interests.' As I said the words, I knew I didn't want to go, that the idea of slinking off to England after less than three weeks would feel more than simply unfinished business.

Marina rocked onto two legs of her chair in a manner that would have had me telling Maddie off and warning her about breaking her neck. 'The way I see it, you're doing Ronnie a favour because she doesn't want Nadia living here watching her every move. But you, Beth, have to stop thinking that your husband drama means that you can behave how you like. I know that sounds harsh, but the best technique to move on from an unsatisfactory marriage – I've survived three, don't forget – is to forge your own path with conviction but without requiring everyone to keep cutting you slack.'

Speaking up for myself wasn't really my forte, but there was something about the notion that I was not pulling my weight that ignited a rage in me I couldn't contain. I shoved my chair back. 'Firstly, I'm sorry if you feel that everyone has to dance around me. I can absolutely assure you that from where I'm standing, I've never expected it to be the case, or indeed noticed that it is. I've spent my whole life putting myself last so I could make sure Maddie had a happy stable home and Joel could pursue his career and hop off on business trips at a moment's notice. Secondly, there was no mention before I arrived that Ronnie's daughter might want the apartment and that my being here would potentially be an issue. I haven't caused that. That is a choice Ronnie made, otherwise why would she allow me to be here paying peanuts? So I'm not taking responsibility for that. Stop telling me what to do. Ronnie is my landlady and, to a degree, I'll respect what she tells me, but you, Marina, you're like a nosey neighbour peering over the fence and having a view on how I hang out my underpants.'

I snatched up the plates and marched off into the kitchen. From the terrace came the sound of applause. '*Brava*, Beth!'

I grumped about, banging the crockery into the dishwasher and muttering four letter words that I didn't quite have the courage to go out and shout in her face.

Turning round, I found Marina in the doorway. 'You have spirit! Very good.'

'Don't patronise me. It might not look like it to you, but I'm doing the best I can.'

Ronnie called to Marina to sit down. 'Leave her alone.'

I wanted them to go but wasn't quite sure of the etiquette of throwing the landlady out of her own home. On a normal day, I'd have skulked about in the kitchen ashamed of my outburst, but given that I was pretty sure I'd be packing my bags the next morning, I had nothing to lose. Quite a liberating feeling. I put the parmesan in the fridge, took a deep breath and marched out onto the terrace.

'I'm going to leave tomorrow. Then you can do whatever you want.'

Ronnie shook her head. 'Beth. Don't do that. Really. I will deal with Nadia. You can't throw in the towel so soon. Look how much progress you're making. When was the last time you spoke your mind like that? When you arrived, I felt as though you'd completely given up hope that life could be joyful again. But there's an energy about you now.'

Before I could come up with a definitive response, Ronnie carried on. 'I totally understand how it feels to land in a new country where you're isolated from all your usual support systems, you're struggling to get to grips with how everything works and you haven't yet disconnected from what you've left behind. It's quite disorientating initially.'

Ronnie's empathy surprised me. I'd harboured a suspicion that she viewed me as simply lacking in backbone, a middle-aged 'snowflake'.

'At least it's easier for you to keep in touch with your friends and family. When I first came out in 1978, I worked as a house-keeper for an elderly woman near Villa Borghese. We didn't have mobile phones or email. In fact, my parents didn't even have a landline until a few years after I moved out here. They used to pay our neighbour to let me reverse the charges to speak to them once a month. In the beginning, anyway.' Her face clouded.

I tried to keep her talking. Up until now, she'd changed the subject whenever we touched on her past. 'So have you ever returned to England to live since then?'

She shook her head. 'I've only been back a few times for short trips, when Nadia was at university in England and after she got married. Otherwise, I only went back for my parents' funerals and to sell their farmhouse in Cornwall.'

'Didn't you ever visit your mum and dad while they were alive?' I could imagine Marina doing scorched earth but not Ronnie.

'No. I saw my mother after my dad died and she came out

here once when Nadia was born.'

There was something final in her voice that didn't invite further questioning about her family. I struggled to understand how she could have cut herself off so completely, whatever her parents were like. Moving abroad and never going home again was extreme. I changed tack. 'How did you meet Marina?'

Her face lit up with a smile. 'Marina was my employer's great-niece. She became my pseudo-sister. In fact, I'd never had any siblings and all of a sudden, I had this feisty ally who was – usually – on my side. I was so lucky to have someone who could speak English to me until I learned Italian. I'd have been horribly lonely otherwise. Who knows? I might have given up and gone home.'

That explained the mix of affection, rudeness and solidarity between them. I found myself envious of Ronnie's courage at leaving everything behind and starting again. The bravery of the young. Forty-five years without running home.

Marina raised her eyebrows. 'Ronnie's being very loyal and not apportioning blame for the fact that she met Matteo through me – he was at school with my first husband.'

'Yes, curses upon you for that,' Ronnie said.

'Why do you say that?' I asked, feeling rudely nosey but emboldened by the applause of speaking my mind.

They both fell silent.

Ronnie eventually said, 'I lost myself in that marriage.'

I waited for her to elaborate but maybe no elaboration was needed. Perhaps that sentence contained a raw truth common to so many women. Common to me, at least.

Something shifted in me. I'd never really lived alone, going from my parents' house to university and setting up home with Joel after a brief flatshare in London. Always trying to meet other people's expectations. Prioritising what they wanted me to be without even asking myself the question, 'Is this who *I* want to be?' Life had delivered me the opportunity to find out now.

At fifty years old, it was more than likely I wouldn't get another chance, certainly not one as good as this. If someone like Ronnie, with her forthrightness and grit, thought she'd lost herself, then I should probably snatch the possibility of a few weeks focusing on what I would and wouldn't accept as my lot over my remaining few decades. Perhaps I could avoid my gravestone reading 'Dull but dependable person who never did discover who she was'.

With the rush of adrenaline that comes with making a decision that seemed almost impossible but turned out to be quite simple, I filled everyone's glass and took a huge swig from my own.

I turned to Ronnie. 'If you haven't changed your mind, I'm going to stay until the last possible day, if you're sure it's not going to create a huge issue with Nadia. I would appreciate it if you would let me invite my daughter and my friend out at some stage.'

She nodded. 'That's okay but they mustn't get in the way of your challenges.'

I was so relieved that I could offer Maddie a few days here that I was ready to agree to anything. And despite today's irritation with Helen, I owed her for giving me the push I needed.

Ronnie folded her arms. 'You must go on a date. It doesn't have to lead anywhere, but the simple act of being in another man's company and observing how he reacts to you will change how you see yourself. You can pick someone completely unsuitable, someone with whom there need be no romantic involvement, if you are still persisting with this idea that you want your husband back.'

'That's the whole point of this.' I slumped into my seat. 'I can't just walk out onto the street and find a bloke to have dinner with. Especially one I want to experiment with rather than properly go out with.' I hadn't liked it when Joel had gone for a drink with someone of the opposite sex, however 'innocent' it was supposed to be.

Marina batted the air in front of her as though I was raising unreasonable objections. 'We will find someone for you.'

Ronnie and Marina cackled with laughter as they discussed the possibilities. 'What about Remo's son? He got divorced last year.'

'Nooo. He lived at home until he was thirty-seven. Preferred living with his mother over his wife. Lorenzo, with the garage?'

It was Marina's turn to shake her head. 'No. He likes wine more than he likes women. And his nails... always so dirty.'

And so it went on with a bewildering array of names, coupled with cries of '*No, brutto! Stupido! Deficiente!*'

I wasn't convinced either of them had great futures as matchmakers.

Marina alighted on the one slim possibility I had considered, then dismissed. 'You have to ask the musician. You know where he is.'

My shambolic disappearance without explanation meant there was no way I could present myself at the Giardino degli Aranci. The last thing I needed was any witnesses to my humiliation if he rejected me. But I did have his card. Once Marina knew that, she folded her arms and directed me to my phone. 'No time like the present.'

'I'm not doing this,' I said, despite my stupid brain simultaneously composing a suitable text.

'Stalemate then. We're not leaving until you do. We'll have to sleep here.' Marina got up and started singing an Italian ballad into the night sky, setting a dog barking nearby.

Ronnie leaned forwards. 'She's infuriatingly stubborn. Go on, send a text to see what he says, then she'll leave.'

I protested but tapped out a message, feeling childishly

liberated from all responsibility, the fifty-year-old's equivalent of 'They made me do it.'

The reply came straight back. *I was waiting to hear from you. Meet me outside Metro Barberini at twelve o'clock on Wednesday.*

I showed Ronnie, who nodded her approval.

Marina clapped. Goodness knows how her mother had coped with her when she was a teenager. I could quite picture her shinnying over an ornate balustrade in a skirt that barely covered her backside.

Without any further ado, Marina tottered out singing '*Nel blu dipinto di blu*' with Ronnie bringing up the rear with a gutsy, if not tuneful, chorus.

It was hard to believe that six months ago the most exciting message I received from a man I wasn't married to (or that I actually was married to) was that my car had passed its MOT and my tyres had another six months' tread on them.

8

On Wednesday morning, I decided to leave early to avoid Marina's instruction in sartorial matters. Three weeks in and I was beginning to get the hang of Rome, no longer needing to consult my map, striding down to the river, across the bridge, and through the side streets. I chose a route that took me through Via di Panico simply for the irony of taking a selfie with the road sign. I located my favourite little bar with two tables outside, opposite a church where I could sit and watch the world go by. I indulged my addiction to the little croissants stuffed with confectioner's cream that must have been five hundred calories a bite. I often wondered how the Italians remained so trim despite appearing to exist mainly on a diet of pastry and pasta.

When the church bells struck eleven, I headed to Piazza Navona, where I popped in for a quick gaze at the sheer grandeur of the square. I alternated between admiring the details of the Baroque fountains and watching one particular portrait artist who captured everyone's likeness in a way that rendered them more attractive. I also revelled in the smugness of batting away the entreaties to take a seat in one of the terrace cafés for a cappuccino at five euros a pop because as a Roman native of twenty-one days' standing, I wasn't going to get sucked in by rip-off touristy places. I was already developing an embarrassingly superior 'them and us' mentality, having eschewed shorts and T-shirts and adopted wide-leg flowing trousers and a fine-knit top. With my sunglasses on and my hair clipped up, I was Audrey Hepburn in my mind until I caught sight of myself in a shop window and realised I looked more like a farmer's wife on her way to churn the butter than a film star. With that rather disconcerting thought, I strode on, past the Trevi Fountain. I made a mental note to revisit it at the crack of dawn to avoid craning my neck over the six-deep crowd and fighting through the selfie sticks.

As I approached the Barberini metro ten minutes early, I repeated Ronnie's words to myself. 'Don't think too much. You're not promising this young man anything. You're just remembering that your husband doesn't hold all the cards, that you're not to going to sit around while he sips his Kir Royale in the shadow of the Eiffel Tower and contemplates whether you're worthy of his affection.'

Nonetheless, it didn't stop me feeling guilty. As I waited for Rico, I squared it in my mind that this rendezvous evened out Joel's evening in the pub with a colleague from work. Sort of. Though as Rico approached, in a bright blue suit, brown shirt and a green tie, a colour combination that really shouldn't have worked, I didn't think I could even tell myself, let alone Joel, that this fell into the category of 'not wanting to have yet another drink on my own'. Rico somehow managed to look both smart and as though he'd recently got out of bed, though I suspected the ruffled hair and the stubble were carefully curated.

He did a dramatic flinging open of his arms. 'Hey! You're here. Super punctual, eh? Couldn't wait any longer?'

I had to laugh at his arrogance. His big smile, his pleasure at seeing me felt like hundreds of fairy lights were illuminating me, a total contrast to Joel coming through the front door and frowning if I greeted him when he was still looking at his phone.

He kissed me on both cheeks and said, 'Can I be the boss and take you somewhere? Then maybe we go for a picnic?' He gestured to his rucksack. 'I brought food.'

'I'm in your hands,' I said, then replayed the statement over and over in my head, asking myself whether I sounded too forward instead of concentrating on where he was leading me.

He stopped outside a church. 'Chiesa di Santa Maria della Concezione.'

I didn't know what I was expecting, but religion hadn't been a big deal in my family and churches always made me nervous, as though I was going to knock over a candlestick or stomp over a sacred spot.

Instead of guiding me up the steps to the church, Rico beckoned towards another door. 'Maybe you hate this. But it will make you glad to be alive.'

Within minutes, we were in a crypt. A crypt! At least I'd be in a position to confound Marina and Ronnie's expectations of a fairytale romance. It was a series of small caverns decorated entirely with skulls, pelvic bones and femurs, with skeletons standing guard dressed in Capuchin monks' clothing. I kept glancing at Rico, wondering what reaction he expected me to have, as though he was testing me, to see if I took it in my stride, found it funny or was moved by it. He seemed interested and knowledgeable – 'The Capuchins used to be housed near the Trevi Fountain, but when they transferred here, they decided to bring all the bones of the friars who were buried under the Chiesa di Santa Croce e San Bonaventura with them'. I still couldn't shake the feeling that he'd brought me here as a kind of prank. I was all for the unusual and off the beaten track, but this was bizarre with bells on it.

I had to concede there was a macabre beauty about the

place, with ceiling decorations made from vertebrae, lanterns sculpted from bones, even two severed arms crossed to form the Capuchin coat of arms. One mummified monk stood near a sign that read, 'What you are now, we once were; what we are now, you shall be.' And other cheery thoughts to brighten my day.

I followed Rico through the rooms, overwhelmed by the sheer scale of body parts. 'How many monks are here?'

'About three thousand and six hundred. The Capuchins wanted people to think about dying, and, of course, about their sins and the need to *espiare* – you know, to make better.'

'Atone?'

'Yes, atone.'

We finally emerged into the sunlight.

Rico smiled. 'Did you like it?'

'I found it calm and peaceful. I thought I'd find it creepy.'

He laughed. 'I don't know why, it's one of my favourite places.'

My mind jumped to the headlines in a newspaper of 'Middle-aged British woman murdered after first date in a crypt'.

He nudged my arm as though he'd read my mind. 'Don't worry. I am not some serial killer.'

I was pretty sure that many serial killers had used that line.

'Come on. Now after the dark of the crypt, we need air. Are you happy for taking the metro? There's a beautiful park, Parco degli Acquedotti, but it's quite long. Do you have time?'

Maybe it was the monks' stark warning of 'what we are now, you shall be', but the 'I need to get back' morphed into a 'Why not?' I liked the feel of those words as they came out of my mouth. Spontaneity hadn't played a starring role in my life recently, obliterated as it was by work and family obligations.

Rico wasn't joking when he said it was a bit of a trek, but thirteen stops later and a short walk, we entered a park that summed up Rome for me. A glorious open space tucked against a casual setting of a crumbling ancient aqueduct, as though incredible feats of engineering were commonplace, a scenic backdrop for a can of Coke and a sandwich.

We sat down on a grassy bank.

'Do you take the beauty of the city for granted?' I asked Rico. 'I mean, when you're walking past, say, that building near the Mouth of Truth, you know the one with the double row of arches and then apartments on the top?

'The Teatro di Marcello?'

'Yes, I think so. Do you ever stop to look at the splendour of it, or do you rush past, trying not to be late for work and wondering what you'll cook for dinner?'

Rico considered my question. 'Firstly, I don't ever worry about being late for work because no one notice if I am there or not. Which is sad or happy depending on the day.'

I guessed Rico's work/life balance was better than my racing out the door with a cup of Nescafé in a keep hot cup before my colleagues made a sarky comment about not realising I'd gone part-time.

'But, actually, I do notice everything. I mean, not every day. I'm not always thinking, wow, look at this magnificent arch, but I like to draw as well as sing, so yes, I do appreciate.' He unzipped the rucksack. 'Have I passed your test?'

'I wasn't trying to catch you out. I was genuinely interested.'

He handed me a ciabatta filled with parmesan, rocket and prosciutto. 'Well, you've passed *my* test.'

And despite promising myself that I wouldn't flirt, I leaned towards him, saying, 'Which was?' in a way that invited other tests.

'You've proved you have an open mind, you aren't a hysteric, you accept suggestions without knowing every detail of what is happening. You have, as the French say, *joie de vivre*.'

The unexpected compliment made tears spring to my eyes. To hear Joel describe me, I was the excitement equivalent of fatty mutton in a slow cooker.

I busied myself with my sandwich, but Rico wasn't fooled. 'What? Why does that make you sad?'

I didn't mean to tell him. The husband waiting for me in England was my Get out of Jail Free card. Joel was my 'Oh, I thought you were just being polite and showing me around Rome' escape route, my 'sorry for the mixed messages' sidestep. But Rico was such a nice mixture of teasing, fun and kind that I burbled it all out. I told him all the worst things Joel had said about marriage to me as a mallet blow to any romantic interest Rico might be harbouring.

He waved his hand. '*Idiota*. Let's not speak about this man. You have to show that you can enjoy life without him. Italians understand how love works. English understand football, beer and, er' – he searched around – 'bacon.'

The randomness made me burst out laughing. And from there, we talked about our families – his mother, his father, how they were always asking when he was going to find a *fidanzata* and have some children. I wanted to ask what they thought of his job busking. In theory, I applauded the free spirit, but a small and ashamed part of my soul knew that I'd rather see Maddie in a corporate job with a good pension than singing for her supper and existing hand to mouth.

As Rico explained how he spent the summer busking in Rome and staying with his parents, then disappearing to the Dolomites in the winter to work as a ski instructor – I found myself envying his ability to exist in the moment. I'd be worrying about my knees giving up, about not having savings to rely on, about what might happen next week, next month, next year. Then I remembered I was experimenting with my new impulsive self, a carefree version that I thought might be more to Joel's taste. 'How brilliant to have so much freedom.'

'Sometimes it's lonely. But I meet a lot of interesting people.' He held my gaze until I looked away. I found it hard to see how Rico could stomach the transition from a world of

après-ski and snowy slopes to returning to his childhood
bedroom at the age of forty.

I imagined going to live with my own mum, every six
months, in her flat. Death by doilies and unsolicited advice. I
squashed the image I had of Rico in his kitchen, his mother in
her apron, stirring a risotto. There was something vaguely off-
putting and contradictory about a middle-aged man who lived
with his parents claiming to be a free spirit. Or maybe I didn't
understand family the same as Italians understood family.

He stood up and pulled me to my feet. 'Come on, let's
walk.'

I let go of his hand, the pressure of his grip lingering on my
palm in a way I didn't want to notice. We strolled in silence for
a bit. My mind whirred around how, as an adult, I'd tended to
hang out with people like me, who worked in conventional jobs,
who had mortgages, kids, pensions. The closest we'd got to boho
in our friendship group was the couple up the road who did up
a VW campervan during lockdown, took themselves off to the
wilds of Scotland for a couple of months to 'tick one off the
bucket list' and split up as soon as they got home. Rico's attitude
of going where the music took him inspired an odd mixture of
envy and admiration. An underlying thread of disdain ran
alongside that, however, as though he was selfishly enjoying life
far too much, instead of weighing himself down with responsi-
bilities and thankless tasks like the rest of us.

We passed a big arc of balloons indicating a children's
birthday party. Even the stylish Italians had the requisite ageing
entertainer in a sequinned jacket turning balloons into swords
to a backdrop of tinny music. We watched as two small boys
started a sword fight that morphed swiftly into a kicking and
punching fest and prompted a small army of women to cluck
over.

'My husband was always disappointed we didn't have a boy,
but I'm not sure I could have handled all that fighting.' I was

congratulating myself for the mention of Joel, when Rico led me away from the melee and along a path towards a row of smaller arches.

'So you're a lover, not a fighter?'

I should have kicked that corny comment into the under-growth. While I floundered about for a witty comeback, we ducked under one of the arches. Before we emerged on the other side, Rico put his hand on my arm.

'So? Are you going to answer my question?'

I couldn't look at him. Every choice, good and bad, every possible avenue I'd taken, or could take, seemed to be shimmering under that musty archway. 'I think I'm not going to answer,' I mumbled, fully aware that this was *the moment* that muttony old me had been fooling myself I could put off, flirt with but never have to face. *The moment* that I'd have to confront the confusing muddle in my head that refused to confirm that it was total, utter madness to have a fling with another man in order to prove to Joel what an adventurous person I was. It didn't exactly smack of a foolproof marriage-saving strategy. Perhaps that window of opportunity had closed years ago, long before I'd forced Joel to admit that he felt our union might have run its course.

'Hey.' Rico took a step closer.

I could have moved away. I could have chosen not to breathe in that musky aftershave that made me think of whisky, candlelight and dark bars with couples swaying to soft music. But I didn't. I looked up.

He raised his eyebrows. I couldn't blame it on a star-filled evening after too much wine. It was three-thirty in the after-noon, with the Italian equivalent of 'The Birdie Song' plinking away in the background. My last thought was that this couldn't happen, before Rico leaned forward and kissed me so gently that I had the sensation of remembering something from long ago that I'd never have brought to mind without being prompted. The sort of episode that my oldest schoolfriends would say, 'You were there! Don't you remember?' Then they'd go on to describe how this person fell off a wall and that person drank too much Pernod and black. Eventually, at the very edges of my memory, a long-forgotten landscape would emerge, frustrating in its fuzziness, showing up like a TV programme that you only realise you've seen before as the credits roll.

As his arms went round my waist, Joel's words reverberated around my brain. *'I'm not promising anything.'*

I had promised, though, solemnly and bindingly, twenty-four years ago and the only thing now was to apologise to Rico and walk away.

Today was not going to be that day.

9

The next morning I'd lain in bed replaying the events of the day before, until I felt obliged to get up and examine myself in the mirror to see if I looked different. I studied my face. Nope, still middle-aged with bits that hung rather than sat when my face was in repose. I had lost that pasty English winter pallor and tipped over into the palest tan, but I couldn't claim to be rejuvenated like my divorced friends working their way through Tinder appeared to be. That crease between my eyebrows was still big enough to lose my tweezers down. It ironed itself out by about lunchtime, fading to a shallow crevice, but there it was every morning, encouraging my foundation to clog into its cavernous depths.

I glared at myself. Yesterday was going to be tucked away into the category of things never to be repeated, an action of which to be ashamed. Though, contrarily, also available to be brought out and stroked like an unpredictable cat whenever someone – most probably younger and far savvier with technology – underestimated me. I wouldn't tell anyone, not even Marina and Ronnie, what had happened. If necessary, I would still be able to lie to myself and take the moral high ground when news of affairs filtered round the office. Still join in with everyone having a definitive view on indeterminate facts and choosing sides based on random loyalties rather than any sense of right and wrong.

By ten o'clock, I'd cleaned the apartment, concentrating on feeling guilty about Joel with every sweep of the mop. If I'd been out for revenge, I'd have been delighted to observe that it was harder to tap into than I'd anticipated. Every now and again, I'd have to ignore a little stomach flip as I remembered leaning against the archway, no longer simply a willing recipient of Rico's attention but someone who was high on desire, greedy. In the middle of it all, I'd registered the abrupt end of the entertainer's tinny music, as though the second hand had clicked onto four o'clock and he'd slapped the off button and snatched up his bag of balloons. I'd pulled away, nervous that a whole crocodile of five-year-olds would suddenly start filing past us.

'All right?' Rico had asked.

I'd meant to say, no, not okay. Wrong. Not something women like me who were trying to win their husbands back should be doing. I didn't find those words. I stretched up and kissed him again, and for the first time in many long years, I was completely in the moment, happy to kick my guilt into tomorrow's long grass.

Now tomorrow was here and so was a WhatsApp voicemail from Rico. I couldn't help smiling at that way he had of speaking, the right English words but with an Italian rhythm. His message was short. 'I thought of you as soon as I wake up and I'm thinking of you now. I'm hoping you think about me. In a good way. I am waiting to hear your news. *Un bacione*. To add to all the kisses from yesterday.'

The reminder, spoken out loud, that I had kissed someone who was not my husband brought me up short. I had to put a stop to this.

I ran down the steps to empty the mop bucket into the drain outside as Ronnie drove up on her Vespa, complete with Strega on the footplate. How that dog didn't fall under a bus, I didn't know. Strega waited until Ronnie had kicked the stand down, then leapt off and came running over.

'Strega! No jumping!' Ronnie shouted with absolutely no authority whatsoever.

I was glad Joel wasn't there to see me cuddling and making a fuss of her. He didn't approve of people 'encouraging' dogs and allowing them to do anything other than sit quietly. I loved Strega's enthusiasm for life. Apparently, she was nearly eleven, but like Ronnie and Marina, she'd decided to ignore the march of the years.

Ronnie's whole body took on a questioning stance, giving her the look of a curious meerkat as she came over to me. 'How did it go?'

'We had a nice time, thank you.' I was deranged thinking I was going to fob her off with that.

'And?'

I told her about our visit to the Capuchin crypt.

She shook her head in disbelief. 'I like the sound of him. Quirky. Sure of himself. Only a very confident man would risk that.'

I picked up the mop bucket to signal that I had nothing more to add.

'So, are you seeing him again?'

'No, I've completed my challenge. I've done what you asked.' I ignored the insistent bursts of longing that kept making my heart race every time I thought about the previous afternoon.

'Are you sure? You do have a certain spring in your step.'

And there I was, deluding myself that I was presenting a dowdy, nothing-better-to-do-than-wash-floors face to the world.

'It's not fair on anyone. I wouldn't like it if Joel was going out for the day with another woman.' *Let alone kissing her*, I added silently.

Like a malevolent bloodhound sniffing out a crisis, Marina appeared at the top of the steps. Life at Villa Alba was akin to living on the set of *Coronation Street*, with every neighbour twitching their curtains and commenting on the goings-on. 'What? What's the news? How was the handsome singer?'

Ronnie filled her in. When I said I wouldn't be meeting him again, Marina launched into a 'Don't you put all your eggs in one basket' diatribe, which I suspected might be a recurring theme every time she had a glass of wine.

'I see it differently, Marina. I regard it as being fully focused on saving my marriage, though I can't deny it was a bit of an ego boost.'

'What did I tell you? You're a very attractive and interesting woman. If your husband finds you dull as ditch water, that's his problem, not yours.'

Marina's tactlessness winded me. 'I'm not sure he thinks that, exactly...'

But before I could elaborate, she shrugged, already bored. 'In my experience, all men consider every detail of their lives fascinating, which is why so many women end up doing all the boring drudge. It allows their super-interesting husbands to focus solely on how clever they are and what a lot of value they bring to the family. And what thanks do the women get? As soon as they've brought up the kids and facilitated their mega-important spouses' careers, the husbands accuse them of being boring and unadventurous.' She paused. 'I say get your own back. Celebrate the fact that you can now do everything your exciting husband didn't enjoy, so no doubt you stopped doing it too.'

I wondered if Marina had ever sat on the fence about anything. I envied her the conviction that the way she saw the world was the right way, not one of many ways. My brain was veering between rejecting and accepting her black-and-white view of the male species when FaceTime chirped up on my phone. My heart leapt with hope that it was Rico and dread that the two witches would insist on speaking to him.

'Is it him?' they asked in unison.

It was Helen. I did the 'I must take this' pointing and scampered upstairs.

'Just checking you haven't decided to bail?' blared out of the earpiece as soon as I answered.

I focused on her concern rather than her choice of words, which made me feel as though she was secretly hoping I'd fail.

'Nope. Still managing to hang on in here, drinking coffee in the sunshine.' I flipped the picture round so she could see the blue sky.

'Lucky you. It's tipping it down here.' We had a whole exchange about the weather and work, before she said, 'So, how are you feeling now you've had a chance to take stock?'

I blinked away the memory of Rico, kissing me under the arches.

'This has been really good for me. I do love Rome.'

'You sound like you're never coming back!'

'Of course I am. This is a bit of time out before I pick up my normal life. Hopefully, Joel will realise that it's stupid to throw our marriage away because we've got a bit bored. I'm glad I came here, though – it's not a bad place to be exploring while Joel sits up and takes notice.' I realised that I didn't feel a hollow desperation when I said his name, didn't have that same panicky feeling when I tiptoed to the edge of accepting that he might never come home to me. I wasn't sure if that was progress or not.

Helen raised her eyebrows. 'Well, I'll be glad to see you at work again. Ange keeps shuffling half of your caseload onto me. I thought you might say that you'd hooked up with a gorgeous Italian and were disappearing off to grow lemons in Sicily.'

'No such luck, but Italian men are definitely good for the ego.' I couldn't help myself.

'Better get out there myself then. I could be running around the house naked and Alan would probably still be shouting to me to bring him a loo roll.' She let out the breath of a woman existing in a state of permanent discontent. 'So have you got a little posse paying homage to you?'

'No, not really.' I wanted to tell her about Rico. To have her reassure me that one kiss – or several, but confined to one occasion – wasn't the end of the world.

'Not really? Oooh, sounds exciting.'

'It was one of Ronnie's challenges to go out on a date with someone unsuitable. There's nothing in it, he's just a friend. A busker, actually.' I raced on, feeling myself talking too fast, giving too much away before I had time to assess what might come back to bite me on the bottom.

'Do you think you might have a bit of a fling with him?' Her tone had tipped from mildly teasing to overly interested. I suddenly had a picture of a colleague in the office asking her if she'd heard from me and Helen telling everyone that my husband better watch out because when she'd last spoken to me, I'd seemed quite taken with some street singer. She wouldn't do it maliciously, but Helen was less inclined to consider things private if they made her appear in the know, afforded her some kudos or simply made a damn good story.

I tried to find a reverse gear. 'Oh goodness, no. He's ten years younger than me for a start and took me to see a crypt.' I launched into a description of that and moved the conversation on by asking her if she wanted to visit me for a few days. Her response, 'We're so snowed under at the office at the moment, I don't think there's room for two of us gadding about' was disappointing. We'd discussed the possibility when I was still in England and she'd given me the impression that I only had to say the word and she'd be on the first plane out. She didn't even sound particularly apologetic. I rang off feeling hurt, as well as wishing I'd never brought up Rico in case she started gossiping at work.

I regretted not only mentioning Rico to Helen, but the whole episode with him, though not in the way I would have expected. I'd had a little taste of tenderness, of what it felt like to have someone on my side, someone championing me. Now, alongside my doubts about my ability to scrabble back up into Joel's affections, I was lonely in a way I hadn't been before, almost as though my soul recognised it was deprived of vital nutrients.

Which meant that I was a sitting duck when Rico bombarded me with messages.

Come and have a beer with me in Trastevere.

Help me choose a new jacket at Mercato Monti – we need to give young designers a chance.

You can't leave Rome without trying the pistachio cheese at the farmers' market.

On Sunday, when happy families seemed to be spilling out of every street, reiterating the demarcation between lonely and alone, I caved in. Though I did endeavour to make it clear that we could only go forwards as friends. I blundered through an excruciating conversation of 'that thing at the Parco degli Acquedotti, that I'm sure was just, you know... didn't mean anything. Bit of a mistake.' Mumble, mumble.

Rico had clasped his chest. 'I'm offended now. It absolutely did mean something to me. But' – he held his hands up in surrender – 'I will accept friendship. I have a big and generous Italian heart.' He laughed and acted as though I was making a big deal out of nothing. I chose to believe him, grateful to have an anchor in my untethered days.

During the following week, I clung onto the little markers of time. A Tuesday morning browse around the Feltrinelli book-store. A Friday afternoon trip to Gianicolo Hill, where we sat on the wall in the sunshine, with Rico pointing out all the churches below us. A Sunday outing to the Borghese Gardens to see the water clock. 'Invented over one hundred and fifty years ago and powered by water. Such a clever thing.'

I forced myself to skate around the questions hammering in my mind. Rico never tried again to kiss me, as though that had simply been a test to see how I would react. I convinced myself the occasional arm around my shoulders when he was showing me something was the difference between a tactile Italian and, say, Joel's best friend, Dan. Dan was so terrified I might peck him on the cheek, he walked into our house and greeted me with a sweeping wave above his head as though he was on a desert island desperate to attract the attention of a passing plane.

Ronnie and Marina seemed content to shelve their challenges. For the first few days after they'd sent me on the date with Rico, I'd had an odd feeling in the pit of my stomach every time I saw them, as though they were going to demand that I justified my tenancy by dreaming up something far harder than anything I'd done up to now. No more had been said about Nadia, but knowing that someone was chomping at the bit to jump into my place as soon as possible unsettled me.

However, in a positive turn of events, as Ronnie had predicted, Maddie had had her meltdown and moved on. She rarely even mentioned Joel in her giggling reports of what she and her friends were getting up to. I attempted to strengthen my case for staying in Italy by inviting her to visit during the Easter holidays. I spent ages looking at flights and phoned her with a proposed itinerary, to be met with 'The thing is, Mum...' The thing was, apparently, that her friend's dad ran a glamping site in North Wales and needed a team of people to start getting it ready for summer. 'We can live in one of their barns and he'll pay us fifty quid a day. I don't think I can refuse because I'm absolutely broke. Is that all right? We can go somewhere in the summer.'

The effort it took not to sound like my mum and say in a dejected tone, 'If that's what you think is best, well, I'll manage on my own,' nearly killed me. Once I'd stopped crying into my coffee, I couldn't blame her – camping, partying and who knew what with a group of mates versus missing out completely for the sake of a few days hanging out with your mum. I couldn't compete. I forced myself to be elated that she'd slotted into uni so easily, gobbling up every opportunity that came her way. Not for Maddie beating time until a man gave her the green light for the future.

The knock-on effect was that I relished my carefree existence soaking up the very essence of Rome. Sometimes, I'd revisit familiar places, often returning to St Peter's Square to watch the sun set. On other occasions, I'd investigate new treasures, revelling in the riches hidden behind every façade. One of my favourite discoveries was the Chiesa di Sant'Ignazio di Loyola. I marvelled at what appeared to be an elaborate cupola over the nave, but in reality was a flat ceiling, a painted-on *trompe l'oeil* that was hard to see even when you knew it was there.

As the days rolled by, I relaxed. The matriarchs of Villa Alba both seemed relieved that I was happy exploring, although I made sure Ronnie knew I was prepared to keep my side of the bargain. 'Let me know when I need to do another challenge.'

She'd winked. 'You're already completing one – letting Rome into your heart.'

I decided not to scrutinise exactly what I'd let into my heart too closely.

10

Much to Marina's bemusement, Rome street art fascinated me.
'You've been where? Why do you want to see these horrid
apartment blocks with scribbles by vandals when you can go
and see proper art? Go to the Galleria Borghese and see
Caravaggio. Educate yourself.'

I overlooked her assumption that because I didn't like the
same things as she did, I was somehow ignorant rather than
different. I didn't have the heart to tell her that all those dark
paintings of saints and grim depictions of beheadings left me
cold. Instead, I trekked for hours across the Eternal City to see
ordinary buildings rendered extraordinary by the murals. On
this particular day, I'd found a gem that had made the long slog
over to Piazza del Quarticciolo worth it. I'd sat for ages staring
at *Amore Ribelle* – Rebel Love – a depiction of two young revo-
lutionaries, their tender embrace at odds with their combative
clothing. There was something about the juxtaposition of their
love and the belief that they could change the world that lifted
my spirits. I wanted to rush back to Ronnie to impress on her
the positive effect Rome was having on me. Out of Marina's
earshot, if possible.

But as the gates to Villa Alba swung open on my return, all thoughts of that vanished. Marina was parading about the courtyard barking instructions at Ronnie, while a young man with a shaved head except for a ponytail was setting up a camera tripod. The atmosphere was not one of jollity, with Marina remonstrating with Ronnie, 'Who's going to be looking at you in the photo? The days have gone when we're the main focus.'

Marina's flirtatious demeanour appeared to contradict her words. The way she was strutting about, a little sprightlier, as though her walking stick was a fashion accessory rather than a necessity, defied us to disagree with her assessment. I found it hard to imagine any scenario in which Marina didn't consider herself the main focus.

Ronnie was standing with her back to me, arms folded. 'I don't want to be in any magazine. What if people start crowding out here to see where two mad old pensioners pretend they can fix hopeless women having a midlife crisis?'

Marina raised her eyebrows and looked sideways in a manner that suggested Ronnie might like to look behind her.

Ronnie immediately threw her hands in the air in a gesture of apology. 'Beth, not that I think *you're* hopeless, or even having a midlife crisis.' She shook her head in irritation. 'I just don't want this sort of publicity.'

I asked what was going on to distract myself from wondering if that was how they really perceived me – a sad, directionless failure with my best years behind me.

Ronnie said, 'Marina agreed to be interviewed for a women's magazine – they saw the same advert you saw in *The Lady* – and thought it would be interesting for their readers to know more about why we're inviting middle-aged British women out here to live in Rome for a few months.' She pursed her lips. 'Of course, Marina being Marina didn't think to ask the *owner* of the house if she would agree to be featured and now this poor young Alfie has flown all the way out here to take photos and interview us.'

Alfie looked more amused than perturbed. He'd obviously already clocked that Marina would get her wish in the end.

'I knew you'd be difficult about it. Always cup half-empty. He wants to talk to you too, Beth,' Marina said, as though this was the PR stunt I'd been hankering after.

I shook my head. 'Absolutely not. There is no way I'm having my private life splashed all over a national magazine. I don't need to broadcast the fact that I'm hoping enough of Rome's mystery and magic will rub off on me for my husband to feel reprieved from a death sentence of routine and boredom.'

Marina opened her mouth to argue, but Ronnie stepped in. 'No, Marina. You leave Beth out of it. You're not dragging her into one of your dramas.'

Marina fluttered her fingers at us. 'I'm so sorry for you both. Where is your imagination, your zest for life, your sense of fun?' She waved her walking stick at us in mock despair, one eye on the effect she was having on the photographer.

Alfie had quickly worked out his path to success lay in pandering to Marina's vanity. He began telling her what a powerful image it would be to have the two of them standing in front of this majestic villa, sharing their hard-won wisdom with lesser mortals. 'You make such good role models for younger women – strong, generous-spirited and determined.'

Marina was all giggly, in contrast to Ronnie's stony face.

'Can you imagine what Nadia will say if she sees it?' Ronnie asked.

Marina drew her chin into her chest as though Nadia daring to have an opinion was an outrage. 'It would be a blessing if Nadia sees it. She'd never find it in herself to help anyone out in' – she waved her hand towards me in a theatrical gesture – 'such a selfless and positive way.'

I saw it straightaway, that cloud of annoyance across Ronnie's face, the maternal defences on automatic. Lesson number one, Marina. Mothers can criticise their own children, but God help anyone else who casts aspersions.

Marina ignored Ronnie's objections, continuing to strut about, telling the photographer exactly how the sun moved round to show the wisteria off to its best advantage. She helpfully pointed out a low wall for him to stand on, so he could snap her from above. Marina might not be of the Instagram generation, but she knew a thing or two about avoiding a double chin.

She turned to Ronnie. 'I tell you what. If you agree to do this, I will allow that dreadful Federico, whose son owns the property renovation company, to take me out for dinner. I will make it my purpose to jump you to the top of the queue to sort out the other apartments.'

I sensed Ronnie's interest pique. 'You're going to lead Federico up the garden path, pretending you are interested in him, so he will force his son to make my bathrooms and kitchen a priority?'

Marina opened her eyes, feigning childlike innocence. 'I will walk up the garden path, and if he chooses to follow, who am I to tell him to mind the steps and not to fall in the fish pond?'

While they debated back and forth, I slunk off upstairs to avoid getting dragged into their dispute.

By the time I walked out onto my terrace, the photographer was positioning them in the courtyard, with Marina issuing instructions about the best angles to ensure they looked slim. 'We don't want to play into the stereotypes of big Italian mammas. We need to look stylish,' she said, fiddling about with Ronnie's hair until Ronnie swatted her off.

'Right, one, two, three, say "CHEESE",' Alfie said.

All I could hear was Marina drowning out Ronnie's 'CHEESE' with 'SEX' before finding herself so funny, she kept dissolving into cackles of laughter.

Infuriating and dictatorial as she was, it was impossible not to admire her *joie de vivre*. I hoped it was contagious.

11

By the time Easter rolled around on the second weekend of April, I hadn't quite mastered Marina's unbridled merriment, but I was experiencing a baseline of joy, like an old friend I hadn't seen for ages and mourned not arranging to meet sooner. A short WhatsApp from Joel arriving out of the blue on Easter Sunday soon shattered that illusion. *Project finished early – unexpected two days off this week in lieu of working Good Friday. Got flight reserved to Rome for this Thursday. Shall I press the button?*

No kisses, though? Significant? Or Joel in a hurry?

Delight that he wanted to visit and the ensuing hope for our future mingled with an odd territorial sensation. I didn't want him trampling through this new phase of my life, his dirty boots of opinions sullying the experience by not understanding why I loved the places I loved. And he hadn't said whether he expected to stay with me – and if he did, would that be in my bed or on the sofa? I bristled that, at fifty, I was even having to consider these things. I was supposed to have nailed all of the answers by now. Instead I was stumbling about like a sixteen-year-old trying to get a handle on the basics of social interaction.

I needed to talk to Ronnie before suggesting that Joel could stay at Villa Alba. I wasn't prepared for how overjoyed she would be that he was coming to visit.

She raised her arms in triumph. 'See! He's racing out to keep an eye on you. Don't make it easy for him. Don't sound needy.'

Marina, with her sixth sense for the slightest hint of drama, appeared in the apartment and snatched Ronnie's glasses off her nose so she could read Joel's text. 'Don't make it seem as though you're particularly bothered about him coming.' With her usual bluntness, she added, 'It's hard to understand if it's an "I'm coming for a coffee and a visit to the Colosseum as I've got a couple of days to fill" or "I simply can't last a moment longer without holding you in my arms."' She handed Ronnie's glasses back. 'Are you inviting him to stay here?' she asked.

'That's not really my call to make. I don't want to take advantage,' I said, turning to Ronnie. I felt the same excruciating embarrassment as the first time Joel and I had slept overnight at my parents' house. That whole 'We might be in my bedroom doing things that you'd rather not know about.'

Ronnie shrugged and said, 'No problem for me. Marina and I would quite like to meet Joel and see who it is giving you the runaround.'

Marina wrinkled her nose. 'Men are usually disappointing. My expectations are low.'

I thanked Ronnie and spent the next hour composing a text in line with her non-needy diktat. *It would be good to see you. What's the plan regarding accommodation?* I did the whole kiss, kiss emoji, delete, reinstate, delete.

Keep cool, Beth.

An immediate reply. *I was hoping for a bed at yours?*

I resisted the urge to clarify whether that meant a separate bed, sofa or mattress on the floor. How did this even become my life?

. . .

Four days later, I waited for Joel at the airport, smoothing the embroidered neckline of the boho tiered dress that Ronnie had picked out for me at the Porta Portese flea market. I looked down at the platform-soled boots with zips up the front that I'd bought in one of the vintage shops in Monti. Whenever I wore them, they made me feel kickass and up for adventure. Now, though, I felt like mutton dressed as lamb. I shouldn't have allowed Ronnie's enthusiasm to sweep me along. Joel would think I'd completely lost the plot.

I took a deep breath, remembering Marina's words – 'As soon as he comes out, he has to be hit in the face by the fact that you haven't been letting the grass grow under your feet. Six weeks in Rome has to count for something.' If nothing else, he'd see that I was changing. Trying to change, anyway.

All around me, extreme emotion rose and ebbed as mothers flung themselves on their returning children with an intensity I wanted to disparage but knew I'd be the same. Grandparents leant down into prams, clucking and cooing over babies, swinging toddlers into their arms. A group of friends next to me cheered as one of their own emerged, dreadlocked, suntanned – the epitome of a young man who'd never yet had to think, *I'd better take my nose ring out for work.*

My people-watching came to an abrupt end as Joel materialised. My nervousness was on the wrong side of excitement, fear of being found lacking obliterating the thrill of our reunion after all these months. The first thing I noticed was his bright white trainers, which I immediately wanted to scuff up so he didn't stand out as a tourist. That Meatloaf T-shirt. Marina would need her smelling salts. I'd become such a snob in a short time, but I'd never be able to look at Joel's collection of concert T-shirts in the same way. I'd get him into a plain black V-neck before his stay was over.

I stepped to the side of the main thoroughfare and let him come to me. I was suddenly aware that I was nearly as tall as him in my boots. I had no idea of the etiquette for greeting husbands who might no longer belong to you.

He threw his arms around me, pulling me into a hug. 'Beth!'

I wasn't sure if it was the height of my boots or the fact that on that one day two weeks ago I'd cuddled an entirely different man, thereby breaking our natural mould, but whatever the reason, it wasn't the smooth welcome I'd rehearsed in my mind, more a clashing of shoulders and bumping of feet.

Joel stood still, looking me up and down. 'Rome obviously suits you,' he said and the urgent striving for approval drumming through my body settled.

We walked to the train, with me taking every opportunity to use the little Italian I'd picked up – *grazie, signore, prego, signora* – in the hope that I'd be giving off international-woman-about-town vibes. I guided Joel to the correct platform, showed him how to punch the ticket, told him how many stops it was before we had to change for Roma San Pietro.

'You know your way around.' A little dart of satisfaction rippled through me.

Without his constant jibes about my terrible sense of direction – 'Beth could lose herself in a paddling pool' – I'd realised that I was perfectly capable of working out how to get from A to B. I'd made some mistakes, boarded a few wrong buses, but with no Joel rolling his eyes, I'd simply told myself that I'd seen a bit of Rome that I'd otherwise have missed.

The conversation to our destination was careful and considered, as though we were both feeling our way down a pitch-black hallway in anticipation of a sudden trapdoor. I'd expected to have a torrent of questions bursting to get out, about Paris, about the job, about what communication he'd had with Maddie, how often he'd been back to our home. I couldn't work out whether I didn't want to address any realities yet, but instead I found myself talking about Rome – the restaurant around the corner where the priests sat slurping up their spaghetti, the nuns glued to their iPhones like the rest of us, the fantastic murals in ordinary suburbs by Blu, the Italian equivalent of Banksy.

'I didn't know you were a fan of street art.'

My heart danced with joy at the surprise in his voice. I scrolled through my phone to show him what I'd seen. 'This is quite clever. All the waterslides lead to a cesspit apart from the one belonging to the politicians and the powerful. It's supposed to represent a criticism of capitalism. It's huge, eight storeys high. It was so weird, it was just painted on the side of an ordinary block of flats with everyone's laundry hanging a few metres away.'

Joel gave my photos a cursory glance. I was in danger of becoming that person who tells you at length about the plot of a book you have no intention of reading.

'We can go and see it if you like?'

He murmured noncommittally, 'I probably only have time to see the main tourist attractions. Have you been to the Vatican?'

'I have.' I squashed the image of Rico pointing to Sardinia in the Gallery of Maps and teasing that he'd like to go and spend a month with me there, drinking wine, cooking squid on an open fire and swimming in a crystal-clear sea. 'The museums are stunning, incredibly opulent. You should definitely take a tour.'

'Aren't you going to join me?'

'Of course, if you'd like me to.'

'I did come out to see you, not Rome, although it sounds like a lovely city.'

I experienced a little flip of relief that the purpose of his visit was to see me. A whoosh of fear followed that perhaps this was the final double-checking he wasn't making a grave error before he launched me out of his life.

As we walked up to Villa Alba, Joel gave me all the detail about who his boss was, who he reported to, who reported to him. I had the disloyal thought that Marina's comment about men finding the minutiae of their own lives fascinating was strangely accurate. He barely paused for breath when I pointed out my favourite bakery and exchanged greetings with the mechanic who worked at the little garage I walked past every day. I indicated the bus stop for transport into the centre – 'if you want to head out on your own.' I kept repeating Marina's mantra to myself that I should impress on him that I'd embraced every minute of my trip and if he wasn't careful, the gap he'd left would be easily filled.

'Ta-dah! Here's my humble abode.'

I had the deep satisfaction of Joel's eyes flying wide open. 'Wow. That's a proper Italian mansion.'

I led him up the stone steps, apologising for the banging emanating from upstairs. 'The owner is renovating two other apartments at the moment.' I'd save my stories about Marina for later, served up with wine. She'd obviously kept her promise to go out to dinner with poor deluded Federico, judging by the posse of plumbers who had turned up in the last week.

'This is really nice,' Joel said as I showed him in. 'Crikey, is that the Vatican in the distance?'

I nodded, all proud, as though the fabulous location of my apartment was down to hours of intelligent internet trawling rather than the result of a broken heart propelling me into an unorthodox set-up that happened to work out. It was so unusual for anything I did to elicit an astonished reaction from Joel, that I felt quite giddy. 'Let's have a drink on the terrace,' I said, throwing open the kitchen doors. 'Peroni? I've got some local wine? Or Aperol spritz?'

'That's all very cosmopolitan but I'll stick with beer, thanks. You're obviously buying into "When in Rome". . .'

'I certainly am. Didn't see the point in coming here and not sampling everything the city has to offer. I'll have to take you down to the Jewish quarter to try the artichokes.'

Joel grimaced. 'I'm not sure I've ever eaten artichokes. They always look a bit tough to me.'

'Not if they're cooked properly. They also do fantastic oxtail here.'

I wondered if I was overstepping the mark and becoming a bit too 'look at me with my adventurous new life'. I didn't want my eagerness to impress on him how intrepid I'd become to translate into a desperation to please.

I'd planned Joel's two days with me down to the nth degree. I had a precious forty-eight hours to convince him that there was still so much there, so much worth saving and there was no way uncomfortable silences and questions that were too difficult to ask were going to spoil it.

I brought out some beers and we settled down at the table, with Joel murmuring appreciative comments about the view. 'Much sunnier here than Paris.'

I avoided making a joke about how our marriage was in such a dire state we'd had to default to talking about the weather. 'I've been lucky. I've loved having breakfast outside every morning. Somehow a coffee and yoghurt overlooking the Vatican seems a step up from All-Bran and PG Tips with next door's pug barking at every car that goes past.'

'Sounds like you won't want to come home?'

I felt as though I had an earpiece with Marina and Ronnie issuing answers. *Tell him that you haven't decided what you're doing next. That the time apart has made you reconsider how you want to live. Don't let him think the decision is all his and you're a passive bystander waiting to be informed whether he's in or out.*

'Obviously it depends on what happens with us, but I'm not going to spend the rest of my life commuting to London Bridge to find increasingly clever ways to save tax for people who can afford to pay it. I'd forgotten how much I love art and architecture.' I wasn't sure I'd have the courage to hand in my notice but it was worth fantasising about it out loud, just to see the shock on Joel's face.

'But you'll get such a good pension if you stay there.'

This was the man who'd been telling me I needed more spontaneity.

'I'm not prepared to spend the next seventeen years doing something that bores me. You know, carpe diem and all that. You've always taken the jobs you've wanted, whatever the cost to the family.'

Shock flashed across Joel's face. For nearly two decades, there'd been an understanding that his career was more important than mine. My role was to maintain a steady ship and the accompanying stable income so he could chop and change or take a project at the other end of the country, leaving me to juggle work with Maddie. He'd often get made redundant – which I suspected was an easy way to draw a line under his 'bad fit for the team'. On other occasions, he'd walked out because they didn't appreciate his brilliance, or the management 'couldn't organise a piss-up in a brewery'. I wasn't quite sure why I'd accepted that now. Why I'd assumed that it was my responsibility to keep plodding along, making sure we could keep our marital home afloat.

Joel leant forwards on his elbows, his brows knitting together. 'I think that's a bit unfair. I mean, I've always had much greater earning potential, so it made sense for me to grab every opportunity that cropped up.'

'Potential' was the operative word. But now wasn't the moment for that argument. Joel had always differentiated between what he considered my nice-to-have wants versus his unassailable, non-negotiable needs.

I took another sip of my drink. 'Anyway, whatever,' I said, sounding like Maddie. 'The point I'm making is that I'm seriously thinking about changing career. I haven't investigated possibilities yet, but maybe something in events organisation, perhaps for museums or the National Trust, where I might get to enjoy some art, or at least spend time in some beautiful old houses.'

'I can't remember you being very interested in that sort of thing,' he said, narrowing his eyes as though he was straining to recall the person I used to be.

'I did Art A level. I used to go to galleries and museums nearly every weekend when we had our first flat in London.'

'I remember you taking me to see some godawful exhibition at the Tate Modern. Stuff that any three-year-old could do. But as far as I can recollect, we used to go cycling at weekends.'

I didn't want to pursue the history of that: Joel's obsession with exercise and the implication that any resistance to going out on the bikes or spending Saturday and Sunday mornings on a rowing machine was an indication of my laziness and lack of get-up-and-go. 'Come on, come on. You've been sitting at a desk all week.' Somehow, by superior osmosis, I'd absorbed his interests rather than sharing mine.

In that moment, I wasn't sure whether I was more annoyed with him for dismissing what mattered to me or my own weakness for allowing it to happen. Never too late to draw a line in the sand. 'Why don't we go to the National Gallery of Modern and Contemporary Art here? It's supposed to be really good. Expand our horizons and all that...'

Disbelief flashed across Joel's face that I wasn't letting him take charge of the itinerary and that I'd suggested something that I might enjoy more than he.

Old habits died hard, though. I immediately offered to curtail my fun to appease him. 'We can just pop in for half an hour. It's got a lovely café, apparently.'

He nodded. 'Okay. If we have time.'

I understood immediately that it wouldn't happen. I

wavered between acknowledging that he only had two days to see what interested him and refusing to accept that Joel never had to compromise. I stepped away from pressing the point, terrified of backing him into any corner that might lead to a much greater finality than a refusal to go and look at a few paintings.

I leapt up. 'I'd better introduce you to Ronnie. I said we'd drop by before we go out to dinner.'

Leading him along the hallway, I felt as though I was presenting my new boyfriend to my dad for the first time. I was nervous that if Ronnie didn't like him, she might give up on me for being so keen to win him round.

Ronnie flung the door open. 'Joel! How lovely to meet you. Come on in.'

I'd never tire of her apartment with its exposed brick walls, terracotta floor and, the thing I loved most of all, the turquoise tiled countertop and floaty curtains. The whole ensemble gave the kitchen an air of a stage set for happy occasions and welcoming people. I hoped one day I'd get to have a nose around the bedrooms downstairs.

Joel's obvious awe at the surroundings provided me with a vicarious satisfaction. A bit less so when he started banging on about the use of space and natural materials, as though he was on first-name terms with Britain's finest designers rather than two-for-one money-off deals on Homebase paints.

'Ronnie's husband was an architect,' I said, under the guise of simply contributing to the conversation, rather than warning him to rein in the grandma-sucking-eggs scenario.

Ronnie was charm personified, asking how he was enjoying Paris, reminiscing about her time there, not giving any indication that she knew that things were difficult between us. She waved us off to dinner as though we were love's young dream instead of a desperate wife trying to persuade a reluctant husband to grant their relationship one last roll of the dice.

We strode down to the river through St Peter's Square, with Joel making all the right noises. A month and a half of walking for miles every day had rendered me fit and full of energy. I even found myself becoming weirdly competitive, my new-found athleticism making me want to steam along a little too fast for Joel's comfort and, ridiculously, for my own. I couldn't imagine sitting in front of my computer for eight hours a day any more.

He took a selfie of us against the bridge, with all the lights twinkling in the background. He showed me and, for once, I didn't feel the need to tell him to take another one, to be critical of my chins, my wrinkles. After so many weeks of shopkeepers snatching away any clothes I picked up and saying, 'Too small/too short for you' in scenes straight out of *Pretty Woman*, I'd become quite thick-skinned.

'Shall I send it to Maddie?'

I shook my head. 'I don't want to give her false hope. I didn't tell her you were coming. Did you?'

'No.'

That bald, short answer, even though I'd done the same, chipped away at my optimism.

We walked in silence. I had no idea what he was thinking, which made me feel intensely lonely. It was as though all those nights breathing inches away from Joel, the instinctive, undiscussed routines of our marriage counted for nothing.

At the precise moment that I needed to be my most entertaining, fizzing with the verve he'd accused me of lacking, a wave of weariness washed over me. I steered us into another avenue of conversation, asking about his favourite hang-outs in Paris. I was relieved when the narrow streets of Trastevere opened up, the hum of the bars and the sheer vitality of the area lending us its energy.

My big takeaway from Rome so far was that being able to eat dinner outside in springtime, albeit with heaters and coats, was a gift that the Italians took for granted, like people who never had to diet, or who could pick up any racquet and know they'd make contact with the ball. They didn't bow down in gratitude because they'd never known what it was like to be shut inside for months on end, praying for the first sight of daffodils to signal the end of an unrelenting winter.

I led Joel through the various twists and turns of the streets, pulling him out of the path of taxis squeezing down tiny alleyways, relaxing into the hubbub of the chatter from the taverna terraces. I pointed to a huge restaurant in a square next to Santa Maria in Trastevere, where people were queuing at a lectern before being directed into various lines according to how many people were in their party.

'I thought you'd booked somewhere?' Joel said, reminding me how regimented we'd been at home, how any 'leisure' had to be scheduled into a rigid timeframe that didn't allow for standing idly in beautiful squares, soaking up the atmosphere, the vibrancy of daily life, Roman-style.

'The queue moves really quickly. Especially if there's only two of you. It's worth the wait. I promise.' I felt my confidence about my choice ebbing away. I'd wanted to show him how down with the locals I was, but as I glanced around, there were loads of tourists too. I reminded myself to have faith, that Rico had recommended it, so it wouldn't be a total disaster. I hadn't seen him since I'd known Joel was coming out and I experienced a sudden stab of panic that we might bump into Rico here. I countered the thought with the fact that there was nothing going on between us, so there was no shame in having dinner with my husband wherever I chose, without flagging it up or asking anyone's permission.

Joel started fidgeting. 'I hope we can get a table inside? It's a bit chilly.'

I was all about sitting outside whatever the weather, so when we were called to a table on the terrace, waiters weaving in and out with plates of spaghetti as big as washing-up bowls, my enquiries about space inside were half-hearted. I did a mental high kick at being told we'd have to wait another fifteen minutes.

Joel shrugged. 'Up to you.'

'You can have my scarf,' I said, following the waiter to our spot under the awning. I ignored Joel's huff of annoyance at not getting his own way.

Next to us was a family of at least three generations, if not four, complete with a couple of toddlers who were being passed from one grandparent to another, with a tag-team of crying. Joel was muttering about bedtimes and routines and it being unfair on other diners.

'I would have loved it if we could have taken Maddie out with us when she was little. So much better than that stress of getting her into bed before the babysitter came and the whole nightmare with taxis, terrified of being ten minutes late.'

Joel looked at me as though I'd grown two heads. 'You were totally rigid about Maddie's bedtimes. We didn't go out on New Year's Eve for years.'

I didn't know how to explain without sounding accusatory that Joel had seemed so put out by having to consider Maddie's needs. He'd effectively wanted a life with a child between 8 a.m. and 7 p.m., and for me to be a wife, not a mother, outside that time. As a result, getting Maddie to sleep had become the Holy Grail. Otherwise I'd have to suffer the impatient voice floating up the stairs, 'Are you coming to watch this film or not?' Or the slamming down of the knife if she started crying in the middle of dinner, as though having to break off eating lasagne to comfort a toddler signalled the end of the world.

Because this was marriage, and quite a long one now, I knew he'd remember it differently. He would have dressed up his resentment and stashed it under the umbrella of concern for my welfare and a desire to spend quality time with me. As if any couples with kids under five had quality anything. Most of us were just hanging on by our fingertips and hoping our spouses would still vaguely recognise us as the person they'd married when our offspring were old enough for school.

The waiter swirled towards us, delivering a mind-boggling number of plates to neighbouring tables as well as our wine, scribbling down our orders and flitting off again.

Joel raised his glass to me. 'To our futures, whatever they might be.'

I blew out discreetly, hoping to dislodge the ball of sadness that was gathering in my chest. I fought the sense of not having done what I wanted for years, yet Joel still looking back over our lives and wishing I'd been different.

But crying into my carbonara about past hurts wasn't going to convince him that we had a glittering future.

As the waiter arrived with a pan of *spaghetti alle vongole* for Joel, enough to serve half the street, and the traditional cheese-fest pasta – *cacio e pepe* – for me, I had the bright idea of asking him what he was proudest of in his life. I hadn't realised there was a right or wrong answer until he said, 'I think I've always performed well at work and I've been brave in my career. This Paris job should really take me to the next level.'

Thankfully, his splodging tomato spaghetti down his shirt gave me time to close my mouth again. Apart from the obvious self-delusion about how he'd excelled in every role he'd taken, I could not fathom a response that did not somehow include our daughter. It felt like a personal insult.

'Really? More than Maddie?'

Joel forked up a clam. 'They're two different things. Without the job, I wouldn't have been able to provide such a good standard of living, which meant we could buy a house in a decent area, with good schools.'

It was like watching a film where I'd read the wrong blurb

and was waiting all the way through for Ryan Gosling to appear, but instead there were only ships and sharks.

'I did contribute as well,' I said, making my tone light. I resisted the temptation to mention the long period of unemployment when Maddie was about ten when my promotion had enabled us to keep paying the mortgage.

Joel topped up our wine. 'How about you?'

'Maddie, without a shadow of a doubt. She's a kind, decent human being and I think she's a great addition to the world.'

Joel laughed. 'She is a bit dramatic, though.' Helen had said the same. I'd have to be more careful about what I shared about her going forwards.

'Weren't we all a bit of a rollercoaster of emotions at her age? And she's had to deal with a lot of uncertainty.' I left the 'caused by you' hanging.

I reminded myself that I was here to woo my husband back, not to get out my chalkboard and tally up marital wrongs.

'Leaving Maddie aside, I think I'm proudest of coming out here on my own and not only surviving, but really thriving.'

Joel's eyes narrowed. 'And how has that manifested itself?'

Management-speak was always Joel's default when he wanted to appear clever, or put whoever he was addressing at a disadvantage. Maybe because I was on home turf – I loved that I even considered it like that – I didn't feel inclined to play along. 'It's *manifested* itself in lots of ways. I've spent loads of time by myself and have learnt to enjoy my own company. I never used to go for a walk alone, or even a coffee. I don't get as panicky when I have to go somewhere new. I'm standing up for myself a bit more – you can't be a shrinking violet around Ronnie and Marina.'

'So what you're saying is that if we do decide to live together again, I'd better watch out?' He sucked his lips into a smug expression as though he knew I'd revert to my old doormat self once I returned to England.

'Yes. I think that's it in a nutshell,' I said, smiling to take the sting out of my words, but still enjoying the sensation of putting Joel onto the back foot.

'And has anyone encouraged this change in you?' His tone was neutral but the colour still rose in my face.

'I'd like to think that I'd have got there under my own steam, but Ronnie and Marina are quite the feisty duo, if that's what you mean. And Helen, that I work with – do you remember her? You met her at the Christmas do, with her husband, Alan. She persuaded me to come out here in the first place.'

'I didn't know you were that friendly with her.'

'Our—' I searched for the right word. 'The blip in our relationship has divided my friends into two camps. Some of the ones I thought would do their best to help have disappeared as though they're terrified that husbands heading for the hills – or Paris, anyway – might become contagious. Helen saw me at work every day and realised that I was at a bit of a crossroads, so she encouraged me to explore some new opportunities.' I tailed off, suddenly remembering that I was supposed to be presenting myself as independent and self-reliant, not a wife who needed a shove in the right direction from a more dynamic friend.

Joel finished his spaghetti. With a raise of an eyebrow and a nod from me, he reached over to help with mine, one of the many predictable patterns embroidered into the tapestry of our relationship. That tiny gesture made my eyes smart. That knowing without speaking that builds and filters through the years, the who does what, when and how falling into a natural rhythm. Could we – or did we want to – consign that to history? It would be like deleting a Wikipedia entry of an individual marriage at a stroke.

Joel dabbed his mouth with his napkin, his eyes darting about as though I'd already overloaded him with superfluous details about dreary work colleagues. 'So have you fallen under the spell of any of the local men?'

'Hardly. I've only been here six weeks.' My mind filled with Marina's voice, *'Make sure he knows he's got competition!'* In any event, despite my best attempts, the memory of Rico leaning down to kiss me caused me to blush for the second time that evening.

Joel tilted his head to one side. 'You don't seem quite as devastated at the thought of being single as you were in October?'

Anger flared in me, pushing every other distracting thought away in favour of one. 'As I recall, you said you were not promising anything. So, presumably, you expected the same from me? I'm not the one who wanted to call time on our marriage.'

Joel put his finger to his lips, indicating that we were providing entertainment for the tables crammed in next to us. I didn't feel like being shushed.

'So there is someone else?'

With a sense of running up to a snarling dog and prodding it with a stick to prove how brave I was, I said, 'Would that be a problem?'

'Answer the question.'

Joel's eyes were boring into me. I couldn't throw my marriage away on one kiss with a bloke who probably had towers of twenty-cent coins on his bedroom windowsill. 'No. No one else.'

Joel's shoulders relaxed. 'You had me going there.'

I handed my plate to the waiter, undecided whether to feel flattered that Joel appeared jealous, or resentful that he should have an opinion on how I behaved. The fact that I was having some kind of Shirley Valentine escapade at all was down to his desire to change the status quo.

'Shall we have a wander and get a coffee somewhere?' I suggested.

'I thought we could have a nightcap back at the apartment.'

And after twenty-four years of marriage, I was too mortified to ask what sort of nightcap he had in mind. I still wasn't sure if this 'popping out to see how things are going' was a booty call. Perhaps Joel intended to be strictly hands off until the magical eight months of breathing space delivered its verdict. I'd borrowed an extra set of sheets from Ronnie in case a bed on the sofa was required. However, I'd also hedged my bets by buying some whisky and visiting Marina's beauty therapist, whose bikini waxing had led me to question her skimpy vision of my swimsuit.

I walked home caught between telling Joel that he had a choice of sleeping venues and feeling under pressure to magic up a new bedroom trick to impress him. In the event, whisky – the right amount, by luck rather than judgement – steered us into my bed without the paralysing awkwardness I'd feared. And after a day second-guessing each other, neither of us brave enough to demand a cards-on-the-table conversation, sex allowed us to skip all manner of difficult discussions. We colluded in pretending that sorting out our future was as simple as agreeing to live in the same house in the same country again. That it would be as easy as pressing the rewind button to where we were before, a little more appreciative of each other than we had been. I knew the feeling couldn't last as I folded myself around Joel, my face pressed against his shoulder, but it was such a luxury to deceive myself that it might.

12

Daylight and sobriety smashed the spell of the whisky wand. I clearly hadn't stomped hard enough on the Cinderella-type endings of my childhood. Joel had crept out onto the terrace, no doubt answering a few work emails, instead of being unable to think of anything he'd rather do than gaze at my sleeping face and wait patiently for my eyes to flicker open. Keep up, Cinders.

I made some coffee, childishly refusing to glance in his direction to see what he was doing, as though his movements were of no import. Thank God for a time limit of eight months. I couldn't keep up this nonchalant, independent wife malarkey for much longer. As I handed him a café latte, which brought a grunt of appreciation, I wondered whether all long marriages stumbled to this tipping point. Where fear of loss, of change and straitened finances steered many couples to instruct themselves to ignore the battery of slights, of tiny thoughtlessnesses, let alone the big body blows that could sink the marital steamer ship.

'Couldn't sleep?'

'Lots to think about,' Joel said.

I took it to mean he was considering whether I'd ticked the boxes of sexy, interesting, exciting enough wife. It didn't seem to have occurred to him that he might find the egg-timer empty and one less suitcase in the attic by the time he'd finished his pontificating. Apart from a little vulnerability the night before about whether I'd met any men, Joel gave every impression that he was the only person in charge of the decision-making scales. For one mad moment, I wanted to shout, 'Do you know what? I'll make it easy for you if the decision is that bloody difficult. If you're going to be dragging yourself through the next thirty years as a favour to me, rather than because your heart might actually pool onto the floor in a puddle of misery at the notion of not growing old with me, I'm going to save you the agonising.'

But the part of me that held onto hope crushed down my fury. Of all the little videos on a constant loop, I wasn't yet ready to delete the moment from our wedding day when Joel's face had crumpled with emotion at the sight of me. I'd felt chosen. A winner. So instead I said, 'I'll get in the shower first,' as though taking charge of post-sex body-washing was an unde-niable stamp of authority, guaranteed to make him think twice about the verdict ahead.

After showering, I dressed in a pair of palazzo pants that Marina had persuaded me into. They had a pleated flare within the flare, which made me feel both ridiculous and dramatically film star-ish depending on the day. I came out of the bedroom to find Joel, bare-chested, leaning against the terrace wall, talking to Marina, who was shouting down from her own balcony.

'I'm just making the acquaintance of your husband.' She batted her eyelids as though she was a twenty-year-old who could snap her fingers at any man, rather than pushing eighty with a dodgy knee. As self-confidence and style went, she was a compelling role model for Maddie's Instagram generation, who couldn't post a photo without a group poll. I had the urge to rush inside and rip off my outfit, feeling way beyond trying too

hard and not wanting Marina to witness Joel's reaction. But
Marina proved to be the cheerleader I needed. 'Look at you!
Joel, you need to keep a careful eye on your wife. All the men in
the city will be trying to steal her away. Doesn't she look
stunning?'

Joel couldn't have disagreed anyway without her somehow
swooping down to correct his impaired view of the world, but
he nodded and said, 'Very stylish indeed.' He looked back up to
Marina. 'She won't even tell me where we're going today.'

'Joel,' Marina said, stringing out the vowels in his name as
though she was about to lead him to a chaise longue and burst
into Jane Birkin's '*Je t'aime*'. 'In my experience, men love to be
surprised. And I think your wife is getting very good at those.
She's certainly surprised Ronnie and me.'

'Is that so?' Joel asked.

I had no faith that Marina's teasing wouldn't tip over into a
big-mouthed blurt about the challenge they'd set me with Rico.
'Joel, you need to shower, otherwise we're going to be late.'

Thankfully, Marina waved and blew him a kiss. 'Mustn't
hold you up. *Lovely* to meet you, Joel.'

I went in, shaking my head. If Marina could switch on the
charm like this three husbands in and at nearly eighty, I had to
admire Ronnie for staying friends with her – and holding onto
her own husband in the meantime – for the best part of fifty
years.

Every time the gates to Ronnie's palazzo opened in front of me,
I had a little frisson of excitement about what the day would
hold. I didn't take many photos usually. I certainly didn't let
people take them of me. I hated the proof that grey hair was
encroaching on my blonde, the bags under my eyes and the glint
of menopausal whiskers glittering in the sunlight. In Rome,
though, I wanted to cling onto every last moment and transport

all the sights and smells home with me, to remind myself later that I had had the courage to do this.

I snapped pictures of everything. The artisan olive oil sold off the bonnet of an old Citroën. The displays of bread at the farmers' market. The doors – elaborate and solid; graffitied; tucked away in tiny alleyways like fairy entrances into an enchanted world. The courtyards promising a glimpse into an exotic life beyond. The shopfronts – vintage clothes, tailors', picture framing – all possessed a shabby chic. I longed to have the skills to paint, to capture in broad strokes the mixture of chaos and charm that urged me to walk one more street, duck under one more archway.

So as I led Joel towards the Piazza della Repubblica, where I was going to unveil the afternoon's activities, I wanted him to see what I saw. Instead, he trudged along, moaning about the traffic not stopping at zebra crossings – 'You take your life in your hands in this city.'

I told him how Marina stuck out her handbag like a carica-ture of an old lady and marched straight out, saying, 'All that cheese eating has to be good for something. It'll take more than a *motorino* to make a dent in me.'

We had a good laugh about what a character she was, but it didn't take him long to complain that the cobbles were hard to walk on, that he couldn't believe how they let the rubbish pile up. 'It must absolutely stink in the summer. I bet the river isn't too fragrant either.'

He was right, but somehow, his criticism felt like a personal insult. I wanted to defend Rome as my discovery, my safe haven. The place where, after the massive shock of Joel walking out on me, I'd started to haul myself upwards, no longer waking up every day with my failures racing to taunt me, the regrets of what I could have – *should* have – done suffocating me.

Ronnie had recommended the Vespa tour I'd booked. 'It's quite romantic. You have a driver so one of you sits pillion and the other is in the sidecar. You hear the guided tour through earphones, but you're next to each other and you'll see all the main tourist attractions.'

Joel was so enthusiastic that I didn't even object to him photographing me with the stupid hairnet that we had to wear inside the helmets. He chose pillion and I clambered into the sidecar, trying not to worry that I'd unbalance the whole damn bike.

Within minutes, our driver, Gino, was whizzing us along, one of a rainbow-coloured fleet of Vespas. We felt quite the celebrities as everyone stared at our group. Joel kept giving me the thumbs up. We stopped at the Trevi Fountain and our driver somehow bustled his way through the crowd to find a spot for us to do the traditional toss of the coin in the fountain to guarantee our return to Rome – 'Right hand over left shoulder!' I had the sense of pulling a grand adventure out of the bag.

Gino showed us the photo he'd taken, the coins in perfect trajectory over our shoulders.

Joel swung round and kissed me on the cheek. 'That's a great photo.'

Gino beckoned us back to the bike. 'You here for a celebration, a wedding anniversary?'

There was a pause. Joel shook his head. 'No, a cheeky little holiday.' Then he said, 'Twenty-five years next year, though. Maybe we'll come again.'

I couldn't look at either of them and slid into my sidecar, my heart doing a little skip of joy. I told myself Joel was just being polite. But as we toured the sights – the Spanish Steps, the Jewish ghetto, the Quirinale – I found myself leaning into him, reaching for his hand, reverting to those automatic wife actions of picking up his sunglasses, checking he'd got his phone.

Joel was bowled over by the Pantheon and the clever architecture with an oculus in the roof and drains in the floor so the rain could run off. I'd never known him appreciate a church in his life – 'They're always so dark' – but his enthusiasm made me want to run out through the solid bronze doors and hug all the drivers for their brilliance in dreaming up this tour.

Before I knew it, we were off again, rolling through the narrow streets of the Monti area, past art galleries and shops only selling old denim jackets, and terraces where the bizarre and the beautiful sipped aperitivi. I'd swapped places with Joel and was clinging to the pillion seat as we negotiated tight turns and unpredictable pedestrians. I alternated between feeling like the most carefree person in the world and one step closer to meeting my maker.

Through the headset, I heard the guide's voice say, 'And today, there's an added bonus. Because the road to the Colosseum is closed, we're going to take a detour.'

Joel grinned up at me.

As we passed the church with the Bocca della Verità and Gino indicated right, my heart quickened as I clocked which direction we were taking.

'This is the perfect place to see the sunset,' the guide said.

Before I could formulate any kind of a plan, the little fleet of Vespas stopped opposite the gates of the Giardino degli Aranci. Before I'd even stepped into the treelined avenue, I could hear Rico. 'Let It Be' reverberated around the park.

I hung back, wondering how I could avoid walking past. Joel was beckoning me on. I followed him towards the viewing point, oblivious to the beauty of the orange glow bathing the domes and rooftops, the pink tendrils of a spring sunset seeping across the sky, the couples sequestering the stone benches with their rugs and bottles of wine.

As we reached Rico, Joel took my hand. 'It's stunning up here.'

To my horror, he stopped right in front of Rico and fumbled in his pocket for a coin. I had the mad thought that I hoped Joel didn't insult him by throwing in a ten-cent coin, as though two euros would make the difference to what would probably rank as the most awkward moment of my entire existence.

Rico inclined his head but didn't take his eyes off me. No smile, no twinkle, just locking his eyes onto mine with no indication what he was thinking. I did a half-wave. Thankfully, he carried on singing so I didn't have to make a snap decision about whether to introduce them. What would that have even looked like? 'Joel, this is Rico, the man I was kissing in the park a couple of weeks ago. I have a teenage crush on him that makes me feel that every song about love was written especially for me. When you're recounting something, particularly when the point is to showcase your endless talents, I might look fascinated but it's equally possible I've suddenly remembered how much I enjoyed kissing Rico.'

Joel gave Rico a silent clap. 'Great melody you've got going there,' he said as though he regularly conducted jamming sessions in our garage.

I couldn't bring myself to watch Rico's response. I tugged at Joel's elbow, mumbling about keeping up with the group and we walked on. My head was buzzing, a horrible cocktail of shame, embarrassment and regret pumping through me. I was desperate to run over to Rico and clarify that Joel had sprung a last-minute visit on me, and that we shouldn't even be here because it wasn't on the itinerary. But, most of all, I wanted to explain that even though I'd replied to his last text by telling him I was busy until Sunday, I hadn't deliberately omitted to tell him my husband was coming out. Simply that I'd been paralysed by indecision in case he'd stared at his phone and thought, *Who cares? Why's she texting me that? It wasn't like I was gonna marry her. She's just someone I see for coffee.*

So the net result after I'd blown up several million brain cells by overthinking every possible avenue of action – and then inaction – was that there was no way of apologising without alerting Joel to a problem. In addition, Rico's frosty demeanour made me nervous in case he didn't meekly accept my explanation.

I leaned on the wall, listening to Joel twittering on about the view, the lights on St Peter's Basilica, confirming with the guide that, yes, that was indeed Piazza Venezia to the right, with the horse statues – 'Am I right in thinking that Mussolini made his speeches from there?' I should have derived pleasure from his enthusiasm, but Joel could never appreciate anything without having to make someone aware of his brilliance.

We headed back to the Vespas. I took the long way round so we didn't pass directly in front of Rico. I couldn't stop myself from glancing over my shoulder. He launched into 'The Most Beautiful Girl'. I couldn't believe I'd become this person. I'd always despised people who broke their marriage vows. I was totally black and white. 'You're either in or you're out.' Yet here I was, yearning for a definitive commitment from Joel, while keeping the door ajar to a dalliance of my own. Right under my husband's nose. I nearly let myself off the hook by reminding myself that Joel had refused to make any promises, but as my mother would say, 'Two wrongs don't make a right.' Though she also said, 'Never cut your hair short. Men hate short hair,' so her wisdom wasn't foolproof.

We ended the tour in front of the Colosseum. I tried to focus on how beautifully lit it was, how lucky Joel and I were to be in Rome, experiencing such glorious sights. Instead, my heart ached so much that I wished I was staring out over a concrete tower block in a rundown London suburb. Maybe then I wouldn't feel so furious with myself for allowing my sadness – or guilt – to seep into a magical moment.

Throughout dinner, throughout the whole evening, I struggled to raise my game, all the while knowing that being a misery guts would push Joel further away from me. On the other hand, it seemed like a tall order to commit to being the entertainments committee for the rest of my life. I'd be terrified to have a down day in case Joel accused me of lacking oomph again.

Eventually, Joel cocked his head on one side and said, 'You're quiet. You okay?'

'No. Sorry. I've come over really sad.'

'Because I'm going tomorrow?' His voice was gentle, kind.

'That. But also because I didn't think this would be my life. I thought now your parents are dead and my mum's settled, we'd get Maddie to university and we'd have time for ourselves. I didn't expect that you wouldn't actually want to be with me.'

'That's not exactly accurate. I'm not sure what I want.'

All my plans of keeping the conversation light, of impressing on Joel the sparkling version of my new devil-may-care self dissolved. 'So in less than four weeks' time, you're suddenly going to know? Or will you need another six months? A year? Are you going to take another posting? Are you even going to discuss it with me?'

I knew this wasn't how to win Joel over. I could see him shutting off, looking for a way to close the topic down. If marriage to him had taught me anything, crying and shouting never won the day. Which, from his point of view, was a clever tactic because I had to get really upset before I had the confidence to broach anything difficult. Then he refused to engage because he was only going to have the conversation when I was calmer.

I took a deep breath. 'I want to be sure that if we do decide to separate for good, that we've really tried.'

Joel reached for my hand. 'I haven't given up on us yet.'

And with that ringing endorsement of intent, I lay awake till the early hours. I imagined telling our friends we were getting a divorce, monitoring their faces for a lack of surprise, as if the only idiot who didn't see it coming was me. I pictured my mother wringing her hands and spending the next few months apportioning blame, probably in my direction. Comments such as 'Most men don't really like career women in my experience,' would be accompanied by a story about how Dad had baulked at her working one Wednesday afternoon a fortnight measuring out sherbet dib-dabs and pear drops at the corner sweetshop so Mrs Ringrose could get her hair set. I shrank away from visualising Maddie's distress. I did test out my heart's resilience, however, by walking through our house in my mind, packing up our belongings, showing around prospective buyers. Oddly, though, I found it equally hard to envisage transporting myself back to how we'd existed for decades. All those years gravitating towards our places at the table, our ends of the sofa, our sides of the bed, the patterns of matrimony that were never discussed yet nevertheless became carved in stone.

What if this was the last time I shared a bed with Joel? The thing I'd done without consideration for so many years, carelessly, often barely noticing his presence in my haste to pick up my Kindle and have that precious twenty minutes to myself. So many times during that night I wanted to wake him up, to ask him if he was frightened. To dig down into whether he thought it was fear, not love, stopping him making the break, holding us together long past our sell-by date.

I decided not to put the idea into his head.

13

The day after Joel left, I lay on my bed like a Victorian woman with consumption. The me of the vintage markets, trying on fedoras with feathers and fancying myself as a heroine in some 1960s film, about to clatter down the cobbles to a husband who'd finally got a grip, was laughable. I couldn't read, eat or even be bothered to answer the door to Ronnie's knocking. It was as though the impetus that had brought me here had wheezed out, the last gasp of a deflating balloon. I wasn't even overwhelmingly sad, just depleted in a way that no combination of spinach, early nights and Marina's magic fish oils could cure. With Joel still deliberating, I was stuck, unable to plan.

I slept, rousing myself occasionally to make coffee, contemplating a shower, before drifting back to bed and falling into the numbness of sleep, yet never waking refreshed.

On day two, the knocking didn't go away. 'Beth! Beth!'

I dragged myself up and opened the door a crack. 'Ronnie, hello.'

'Are you ill?'

I shook my head. 'I don't think so. More exhausted.' Even my words felt like they were commando crawling into the air. I braced for a lecture about how I needed to get up, get on, do some clever thing that would require an energy that felt so far out of my reach.

'I'm taking you to the seaside. You need a change of scenery.'

I struggled to keep the irritation out of my voice. I longed to be left alone to mope for a while. 'That's very kind of you, Ronnie, but I'm not going to be much company.'

'It's one of your challenges. I'll wait for you downstairs with Strega in half an hour.'

'No. I can't do it, not today.' I sounded snappy and impatient but Ronnie smiled, in that lotus pose and herbal tea way of hers.

'You can. Bring your swimming costume.' She turned on her heel, practically clapping her hands in anticipation of a day at the beach, as though my refusal to comply had gone over her head.

I banged the door shut, not caring if I seemed rude. The not so discreet whispers in the stairwell alerted me to the fact that Marina wasn't far away. Today, they'd just have to be disappointed in me. Join the bloody club.

However, I couldn't outsmart those neural pathways worn smooth in childhood by my mother's refrain. 'Elizabeth! You're a guest in their house!' I was powerless to resist doing the polite thing, as much part of my DNA as my brown eyes.

I grumped over to the drawer and pulled out my costume, collected up a towel and my Kindle and scuffed downstairs. Ronnie was backing an old-fashioned Fiat 500 out of a shed that I'd assumed was a storage facility for her gardening gear. Everything was rattling in a way that suggested it didn't go on many outings. She stepped out and called to Strega. 'You didn't think we'd go without you, did you?' she said, kissing the little dog on the nose.

Marina was lurking in the drive, dressed in a padded jacket, scarf and hat as though she was off on an expedition that involved penguins rather than paddling.

'Ridiculous going to the beach at this time of year. You needn't think I'm going near the water.'

I didn't like to point out that twenty-four degrees in the UK at whatever time of the year would cause tailbacks to the coast.

Ronnie ignored Marina as though she was the noise of a distant motorway. 'Right, Beth, you sit behind with Strega. Marina, pick your chin up off the floor and get in the front. We'll park at your villa. Have you got the padlock key?'

'It's got a combination code now,' came the sulky reply.

I was grateful that those two were sniping away at each other so the burden of conversation didn't fall on me.

After about half an hour, with Strega snoring on my lap and a breeze blowing in from the sun roof, I felt something in me waving feeble fronds of life, a bit like supermarket coriander shocked by being watered and fed. I pressed my face against the window as we left the motorway. A childish thrill ran through me at the sight of the sun sparkling on the sea as we drove through the villages lining the coast, so quiet and deserted after the bustle of Rome.

Ronnie drew up outside a huge terracotta-coloured villa, green shutters closed against the world. Patches of plaster had peeled away, the metal framework for the roof terrace canopy exposed and bare, lending the building an unloved air.

Marina clicked her tongue and muttered about her husband gambling away the money for renovations. I managed to rouse myself from my torpor long enough to appreciate what a privilege it was to see other people's houses close up, rather than peering into their gardens through the railings. This majestic villa was like something I watched on *Grand Designs*, with the host intoning about unexpected plumbing problems and budget-busting roof repairs.

Marina levered herself out of the car and opened the gates. 'I'm not going inside. I'm not in the mood for memories today.'

I squashed the outrage at being deprived of a snoop round the villa and tagged after Ronnie to the beach, with Marina dragging behind.

'There aren't even any sunbeds at this time of year,' she moaned.

'Thank God. We can enjoy the beach as God intended rather than being allocated our one square metre of relaxation,' Ronnie said.

I couldn't get over how few people were about on the long stretch of pale brown sand, not Caribbean pretty but far from the mudflats of my childhood holidays.

Marina waved a dismissive hand at the boarded-up changing rooms along the rear of the beach, built into the wall below the terrace of a closed restaurant. 'See, no one goes into the sea in April. There's nowhere to change.'

Clearly Marina's mother had not peppered her formative years with inadequate towel tents guaranteed to show your buttocks to the entire world at a critical moment and an urging to 'do it quickly, no one's looking'.

Ronnie said, 'Shall we swim, Beth?'

Marina threw her hands up as though Ronnie had taken leave of her senses. 'You'll catch pneumonia. And you only had breakfast a short while ago!'

I frowned.

Ronnie explained. 'Italians think you'll die of cramp if you go in the water within two and a half hours of eating. When Nadia was little, a family who'd sat next to us at lunch told me off for letting her swim straight afterwards and when I didn't do anything about it, they went snitching to the lifeguard to make sure he kept an eye on her. I grew up in Cornwall. We spent our whole lives in the sea without ever getting the fabled "stomach cramp".'

I laughed, but Marina twisted her lips in disapproval as though she'd refuse to call for help if we got into difficulty.

'How cold will it be?' I asked.

'Freezing,' Marina said. 'You need to come in August.'

Ronnie tutted. 'It will be a bit chilly to begin with. But once you're in, I promise, you will be revitalised. It's just what you need.'

The water was crystal clear, but the fact that there wasn't a single person in the sea felt like a sign.

Ronnie stripped off her T-shirt and trousers to reveal a swimsuit underneath. 'I can hold a towel round you. Or if you walk over to the changing rooms, no one will see you behind that pillar. Come on. Don't tell me you never went in the sea at Easter in England as a child.'

Resistance was futile.

A few minutes later, I was striding down to the shore feeling as though the hidden eyes of the whole town were on me. I stopped as my feet made contact with icy water.

'Walk forward with purpose,' Ronnie said. 'Keep going and tell yourself you'll enjoy it once you're out the other end.'

I couldn't let a seventy-four-year-old show me how it was done. I walked, trying hard not to give Marina the satisfaction of screaming, but nonetheless failing to stop the occasional whimper escaping.

'Right, one, two, three,' Ronnie said and dived straight in.

I followed seconds later, the cold emptying the air out of my lungs as I flailed about.

After I'd got my breathing under control, I watched, astounded, as Ronnie did an athletic crawl parallel to the beach, which made my sedate breaststroke plus doggy paddle look a little amateur. She moved with the smoothness and grace of someone who can't remember learning to swim. She reminded me of the three-year-olds who'd whizzed past me, poleless on their stunted skis, on the one occasion Joel had persuaded me that a skiing holiday would be 'great fun'. Fun was not what I remembered.

By the time Ronnie swam towards me, there was no denying that as the cold subsided, an invigorated triumph was setting in.

'Better?'

'I certainly feel wide awake.'

With her hair scraped off her face, I had a glimpse of Ronnie as a young girl. There was something wholesome about her. I could quite imagine her diving into the Cornish sea in her navy Speedo costume, whatever the weather.

She brushed the water from her eyes. 'In the year after my husband died, I drove here almost every morning. The Italians of course thought I was mad. But there's a sanity in the body having to pull out all the stops to survive, so that there's no room for thought.'

'Do you miss him?'

'I miss the life I thought I had.' For a second, the vibrancy faded from her eyes and she looked old, the cold making the wrinkles stand out in her forehead. Within seconds, she was grinning again. 'We often don't question love. We don't ask ourselves whether it's still fit for purpose. I don't know why that is. Perhaps we're frightened of not liking the answer. Sometimes we're too grateful to have been chosen. That was my problem, for sure.'

I trod water, feeling as though I was finally going to under-stand what made Ronnie tick, but she turned to swim away again.

'I never felt enough on my own.' And with that, she powered off towards the rocks, leaving me bursting with curiosity to know more about the circumstances that would have caused this self-contained and plain-speaking woman to be riddled with doubt.

· · ·

I returned to Rome in an all together more jovial mood, re-energised both by my swim and Marina's outrage at our idiocy. I phoned Maddie to tell her about my day, but, predictably, the call went to voicemail. I decided instead to tackle the task I'd been putting off – an apology to Rico for not telling him that Joel was coming out.

I'd been prepared for a snippy response, but he replied that he was used to hiding from husbands. The string of laughing emojis that punctuated the message reminded me that not everyone took life as seriously as me. It was a gift to wander the world shrugging, enjoying, letting everyone else froth them-selves into a lather over detail and drama. Contrarily, I had to work hard not to feel offended that he hadn't cared about Joel being here at all. There was no pleasing me. I half-hoped, as a counterbalance to my over-investment in everything, that if so much of what happened didn't matter to you, you ended up with a series of shallow and meaningless relationships. However, when I revisited all the conversations I'd had with Rico, I concluded that he had plenty of people surrounding him who really cared. Nevertheless, he'd worked out how to sidestep the stress that accompanied all my interactions with my nearest and dearest.

If I ever got the chance, I'd have to study how he did it.

14

In the wake of the heart-stopping swim at Santa Marinella, I suffered the sudden anxiety that I used to get on about day nine of a fortnight's holiday, that it was all a countdown to the end. In reality, I still had three weeks left before returning to England. I didn't want to waste a single minute.

After Joel's visit, I'd planned to reduce how much time I spent with Rico in order to cement in both of our minds that we were truly just good friends. But unlike back home where I could have distracted myself with half a dozen people in any given week, I didn't know anyone else apart from Ronnie and Marina. There was a certain imbalance in those relationships and I definitely had to be in the mood for Marina. With Joel reverting to a few perfunctory texts, I decided the only way to stay sane was to deploy Ronnie's 'walk forward with purpose' with the adjunct of 'one day at a time'. So I pushed down my misgivings and carried on meeting Rico before or after his shifts. Sometimes we sat in companionable silence, sometimes we walked the length and breadth of Rome discussing everything from bucket lists to our favourite flowers. I refused to consider how much I'd miss him when I left, the way his face crinkled with delight when I came round the corner, how he understood instinctively whether to tease me or take me seriously.

In the seven weeks I'd been in Rome, the city had grown noticeably busier. I'd become shockingly resentful when my preferred table in my favourite café was commandeered by tourists who spent their entire time discussing whether it was best to choose the euro or dollar/pound conversion option when the bill came. Rico teased me for becoming more Roman than the Romans. 'Come on. Think about the economy. We need all your pounds and dollars. A good summer for me means I can go travelling in October. You could come with me.'

I smiled and ignored any comments like that, a tactic I'd fine-tuned when Marina shouted over to Ronnie, 'She's going out with Rico again! That challenge is over. We need to move her on to the next one.'

At the end of April, two weeks before I was due to go home, Rico took me to a posh taverna. It was a step up from the spit and sawdusty places we sometimes hung out at, tiny venues like someone's sitting room, tucked away in the most unprepossessing side streets. There was either no menu or the owners disregarded our choices, telling us that the lamb was good today, or they weren't doing sardines but would bring anchovies 'fresh from Ponza this morning' or sea urchin spaghetti. The etiquette seemed to be one of 'eat what you're given'. I lived in fear of not liking it and the cook coming out to remonstrate, so it was quite relaxing to be in a normal restaurant where I might dare to say, 'Could you put the sauce on the side?'

'An old French guy got all emotional because I sang "Yesterday When I Was Young" and it reminded him of his wife who died. He gave me fifty euros, then the group he was with all started pulling out their wallets as well. So *santé, ma chérie*, and to his wife as well,' Rico said, raising his glass.

I had the best ricotta-stuffed courgette flowers and wondered whether I'd ever again be able to enjoy dough balls as a starter with the same gusto as before. As I was tucking into my main course – strozzapreti pasta with fresh tomatoes and basil – Rico said, 'So, two weeks and you find your fate, eh?'

I froze for a second. We usually did an excellent job of skirting around the Joel-shaped elephant in the room. 'Well, I don't suppose Joel is going to fly over on day one and deliver the verdict. I'm assuming there'll be a period at home while we get a sense of what the future might look like.'

Rico twisted his fork in his fettuccine with porcini mushrooms. He didn't look up from his plate. 'And you, you can accept that?'

'I have to, Rico. If I want to have a chance of staying married.' The thought of going home and discovering that my future bore no resemblance to what I'd taken for granted for the last two decades was terrifying. However, even when I daydreamed about Joel bursting through the door, taking me in his arms and telling me he'd been so stupid, I was unable to summon up anything approaching elation, just a dull relief. I was destined to be slightly discontented for the rest of my days.

Rico did that half-smile thing, as though he was privy to information that he was never going to share with me. Whatever was going through his mind didn't feel like a compliment to my determination to fight for the life I deserved.

'You've never been married, Rico. It's different when you've got so much history and a child together.'

'I'm sure it is,' he said in a tone that suggested that, married or not, he'd have been setting his own agenda by now.

I shifted to a different topic, talking about the restaurant, the other diners, how much I'd miss Rome, but the air had squeezed out of the evening.

Rico declined an espresso at the end of the meal and as we walked to the river in silence, his easy jokey manner transformed into something tense. My head hummed with self-justification, fuming that every other person in the whole world appeared to be the expert on my marriage while not actually holding together a relationship themselves. As we came out into Piazza Trilussa, there was a band on the steps, playing Ed Sheeran. When the song finished, the lead singer whistled and shouted. 'Rico! *Vieni a cantare.*'

Rico waggled his index finger. '*No, Marco, stasera no.*'

I just about managed to follow the exchange between them, including the guy signalling with his thumb towards me – *la nuova ragazza?* – asking if I was his new girlfriend. Sometimes I couldn't wait to get back to England, where people would pretend not to be staring while furiously trying to work out where everyone slotted into the equation.

Rico screwed up his face as though that was an awkward question but didn't answer. I suddenly felt as though they were having a joke at my expense, as though there was no way on earth someone as old as me could possibly be his girlfriend.

The guy sang the opening bars to 'Hotel California' and beckoned to Rico.

I tapped him on the arm. 'You stay and sing. I'll get a cab.'

'Betta. Just one song with Marco, then I take you on the Vespa.'

I didn't want to leave the evening on a bad note, so I nodded and stood in the corner of the square feeling as though everyone was whispering about me. Rico did some clever harmony in the chorus and I clapped along with everyone else. When the song finished, I waited for Rico to jump down, but he said something to Marco, who made an 'Are you kidding me?' gesture but gave orders to the rest of the band members.

Marco handed Rico the microphone. Rico said something in Italian, which elicited something between a cheer and an 'Awww' from the crowd. Then in English, he said, 'It's complicated.'

He nodded to the guy on the sax and soon the sweet notes of 'Leaving on a Jet Plane' were echoing around the square.

Rico stepped forward and sang, never once looking my way. I didn't dare assume he was singing for or about me, so I hovered on the periphery of all the people swaying, some with their lighters above their heads, envious of everyone there who appeared to know their place in the world.

At the end of the song, to huge applause, Rico gave a thumbs up to the band, said, 'Like I said, it's complicated,' and bounded down the steps, pointing towards the road.

I caught him up. 'They all loved you.'

He stopped walking. 'It's not "they" that interests me.'

I was making a bit of a habit of standing still, wondering whether I'd got the wrong end of the stick.

'What do you mean?'

'*Porca miseria*, Betta!' He rapped his knuckles on his skull. 'What is your head made of? Wood? I'm jealous, Betta.' He was gesticulating, fingers splayed. 'I don't want you to go back to, *madonna*, your husband, what's his stupid name...'

Despite the fact that I'd known all along that there was more than friendship bubbling under the surface of our time together, I still had the naivety to be surprised at this turn of events. I was such a coward, I'd never broached the subject and I'd somehow expected Rico to be bound by the same fear of making a fool of himself. Stupidly, I'd made the mistake of thinking I could enjoy his company, get close to him, hoover up the emotional support and his generous affection, then leave. I'd assumed that I'd somehow glue a fat sticking plaster over my threadbare marriage. I'd intended to plod on, providing enough bursts of planned spontaneity that Joel would eventually become too old to mind that I bored him half to death. Perhaps he'd dutifully tell the undertaker to engrave my headstone with 'beloved wife'.

But despite all those thoughts charging at me like a play-ground of kids released into the summer holidays, what I actually said was a tiny percentage of anything that could have expressed the muddle in my head.

'I'm sorry. I didn't mean to give you the wrong impression. I thought we were friends, that the whole *parco* thing was simply a one-off. Rico, I'm married.'

'Only sort of married.'

'I don't think marriage comes with a "sort of".'

Rico closed his eyes for a long moment and pressed his lips together. 'Come on, I'll take you home.'

He marched ahead of me until we reached the bike, handed me a helmet and clicked his own into place. During the fifteen minutes it took us to arrive at Ronnie's, I could not formulate what I was going to say to make it right.

I clambered off the bike, removing my helmet. For one horrible moment, I thought Rico was going to drive straight off, but eventually he hooked his helmet over his arm and ruffled his hair. 'Betta. I cannot see you any more.' He tapped his chest. 'I have to protect this.' He leaned forward, kissed me lightly on the lips, jammed his helmet on and disappeared down the drive before I could think, let alone articulate. But, apparently, not before I could feel. Raw. Sore. Bereft. If any of this was about love, I'd be well-advised never to go near it again.

15

May arrived and with it, the countdown to my departure the following week. With superhuman effort, I fought against allowing my last memories of Rome to be dominated by my reaction to a man. So I did what I always did. I prised up the corner of the bunker where I'd stuffed every other uncomfortable event and slammed the lid back down. Apart from first thing in the morning when my thoughts raced out of the starting blocks before I could get them on a lead, I refused to let Rico strum his way into my mind. I directed my vision away from the nebulous longing hovering at the edge of my consciousness, poised to morph into acute sharpness if I paused for a moment and lost focus.

I made myself busy. I started saying goodbye to the city that was supposed to fix me, give me clarity of thought, but had left me more confused than ever. It was astonishing that despite all these weeks, all the endless days to discover, there were still things left undone.

On Tuesday, in a gesture of defiance towards Joel, if not to Rico, I took myself off to the National Gallery of Modern and Contemporary Art. With the carcasses of horses hanging from the ceiling, ripped bits of black fabric and blank white squares posing as pictures, I was grateful that I hadn't had to suffer Joel tutting and huffing. And thankful that I could spend as long as I wanted at the photographic exhibition of the poet Alda Merini. I was obviously a total pleb as I had never come across her before. She looked so comfortable in her own skin, with her pearls, her eyes closed in the ecstasy of a robust nicotine hit as she took a drag on a cigarette. She hadn't shied away from the camera because her hair wasn't immaculate, because the angle wasn't flattering or the sunlight caught the evidence on her face of a life long and hard-lived. I couldn't take my eyes off the photos. Her defiant sassiness. Everything about her said, 'This is me. What you going to do about it?' If Joel had been there, he'd have stopped me from soaking it up in his haste to move on, with no regard for whether another exhibit would be more interesting, just next. I couldn't wait to discover her poetry. Joel would have waggled his head and said, 'Ooh get you, all literary now,' and made me feel pretentious.

I had nothing to rush back for, so I looked at every single exhibit, returning to *Sogni* (Dreams) by Vittorio Corcos. I wanted to be friends with the young woman in the painting. Despite her modest head-to-toe plus gloves attire befitting a woman sitting on a bench at the end of the nineteenth century, she had that look. That steely determination with a hint of sulkiness that promised she'd be no one's fool. That she was playing the game but only an idiot would mistake her compliance for weakness. What she knew in 1896, I hadn't learnt in the twenty-first century.

I headed for home, the images of these two women rebounding in my head. I sat at the top of the Spanish Steps for the last time, watching the tourists on the adjacent restaurant terrace, wishing I could start my stay here again knowing the city as I knew it now, without any wasted days. Any wasted hours. As I made the slow descent down the one hundred and thirty-five steps, my heart constricted as I noticed a crowd gathered around a street singer. Not Rico. I didn't even dare examine what seeing him might have done to me. Instead, I hurried away from the square along Via dei Condotti, which had previously entertained me with its over-the-top exclusive vibe, but now annoyed me. All those pin-thin assistants standing at the doors of the designer shops, ready to block your path if you so much as breathed on their precious shirts. They were probably made of spider web and squirrel fur anyway and wouldn't survive in my house. I insisted that any piece of clothing worth wardrobe room should withstand the handwash cycle on the washing machine. If ever there was an incentive to return to England, it was the joy of being invisible to bored shop assistants who couldn't care less if you squeezed your fat arse into a size eight as long as they didn't have to break off their conversation about their boyfriend's bitch of an ex-girlfriend.

I crossed over the river, eyeing the barrier at the Santo Spirito in Sassia Hospital and the surly security guard. I'd read somewhere that there was a revolving cylinder in the wall where women could place their unwanted babies for the nuns to look after. It held a fascination for me and I'd meant to find a way to see it. Today, though, my limited Italian and fragile heart weren't up to a tussle with authority.

I was running on empty as I walked into the courtyard at Villa Alba but didn't find the sensation displeasing. Physical exhaustion led to less energy for what ifs.

Strega trotted across the cobbles to greet me and I knelt to fuss her. As I glanced up, Ronnie's head appeared over her terrace wall. 'You're here! I've got a surprise guest for you.'

My mind jumped to Rico. I told myself off, but I still didn't wish for the mysterious visitor to be Joel. I'd obviously kicked winching my marriage back onto its feet into the 'to be dealt with when I get home' long grass.

From the depths of the palazzo, I heard a clattering along

the hallway, far too quick for Marina. Out of the front door burst Maddie.

She ran down to me and threw her arms around my neck.

'I thought you were at uni?'

'I was but sacked off a couple of days so I could get out here. All the lectures are on Zoom anyway. I'm flying out on Thursday evening, it was cheap to do two days, I mean, it's not long but...' She shrugged, bored with explaining the detail.

I took a step back. 'Right, great. Well, wonderful that you're here. I see you've already met Ronnie.'

Maddie said, 'And Marina,' in a tone that meant she had some opinions on her. I wondered if she knew she'd had three husbands. At least it made Joel and me look tame by comparison.

'Why didn't you ring me to tell me you were on your way?' I asked, sad to have missed out on the excitement of anticipating her arrival but overjoyed that she'd made such a huge effort to see me.

'I kind of liked the idea of surprising you. If I'd let you know I was coming, you'd have changed your plans, then twittered about me missing uni, and what I wanted to eat and being all mum. I'm an adult now, so I don't need that.'

I decided not to read anything into her words, not to hear 'you'd have fussed about and taken all the spontaneity out of it'.

'Shall we have a drink? It's a bit early, but it's a special occasion.' I still found it utterly peculiar to have a child old enough to share a bottle of wine and often annoyed Maddie by turning into the alcohol monitor. I supposed after two terms at university and a whole Easter living in a barn in the middle of nowhere, she'd have developed a certain degree of tolerance.

She was suitably interested in the apartment. 'This is so cool. Do you think they'd rent it out to me and my mates?'

I didn't want to pour cold water on her enthusiasm, but a bunch of nineteen-year-olds waking up Marina and Ronnie on a nightly basis was not going to happen. Not on my watch anyway. 'I think you'd be better off in Trastevere, where all the bars are. This area is a bit sedate for your age group.'

I passed her a glass of Aperol spritz. She sipped it. 'That's really nice. I feel like I'm in a film.'

I smiled. 'Rome does that to you.'

We bounced from subject to subject – her studies, her friends, the pink streaks in her hair, her discovery of kilo sales – effectively a jumble sale by weight.

'Right, I'm taking you to this second-hand shop I know. You'll love it. I got these brilliant flares...' I disappeared into the bedroom to fetch them.

'Mum! Do you actually wear these?' She sounded astonished, as though she couldn't marry up the woman who flapped about in funky trousers with the mother who nagged about the state of her bedroom.

'Yes. And I bought some Doc Martens there too.'

Maddie swore, then said, 'Sorry, I mean, flipping heck. Last time I looked, you were buying nanna knits from Marks & Spencer. Can I try those trousers on?'

They were, of course, several inches too big on the waist, but she rocked those flares in a way I never would. Nostalgia for my youthful figure – that I never appreciated at the time – sat alongside the thrill of owning an item of clothing that my daughter wanted to borrow.

She sat down, pulling out the pleats and bunching up the waist. 'I could definitely get these taken in,' she said, as though I would automatically hand them over. Which I would. 'So what's happening with you and Dad? I heard he was out here for a few days.'

Curses upon him for letting that out of the bag.

'Oh yes, he popped over to see how I was getting on.'

Maddie wasn't going to be fobbed off with that. 'And? Did

you have a nice time?' She screwed up her face. 'I mean, you don't need to go into any of the weird detail.'

She absolutely needn't have worried about that.

'I'm going to ignore that comment. Yes, we went on a brilliant excursion on a Vespa with a sidecar, saw all the touristy bits of Rome. They showed us this amazing place for ice cream. If you like, we can go down later.' I was glad to have the tour to fall back on, something concrete to report.

'But did you, like, make any decisions? I mean, Dad has caused all this, so I suppose he's got to decide what happens next.'

Although she was bang on the money, I still felt the slap of insult that she saw me as a loser, treading water until the great god of her father uttered his decree. 'Well, I do have some say in it. I mean, I could decide that I don't want to be married to him any more.'

A cloud descended over her face. 'What would be the point of that now? You've been together for so long. I mean, are you really going to start hooking up with randos on Tinder?'

I repeated to myself that my job was to make Maddie feel as though she had a stable, secure and dependable parent, rather than proving to her that I wasn't yet dead from the neck downwards.

'I doubt it. But whatever happens with Dad and me – and I really hope we can work it out – you're very much loved and you'll always have a home with me.'

As if that was as much emotion as Maddie could handle in one day, she nodded and then said, 'Shall we go out for dinner then?'

The next morning, we headed off to the Vatican, with Maddie asking me all sorts of questions about who lived in the Vatican City and how they chose a pope. I had an embarrassingly sketchy knowledge – anything historical or political was more Joel's domain than mine. I had a sudden burst of warmth towards him as I remembered all the times I'd said, 'Ask Dad, he knows about that sort of thing' when Maddie was growing up. I couldn't seem to retain information about stuff I wasn't interested in, whereas Joel was much more efficient at archiving and retrieving stuff that adults really should understand.

Given the fact that I only had one full day with Maddie, I'd paid for fast-track tickets and we were corralled into a line between two metal barriers. Maddie and I got separated as she stopped for yet another selfie. Two teenage girls slipped in between us and I stepped aside to let them pass in front of me.

When we entered the museum, we had to put all our belongings into the X-ray machine and I realised that my phone, which I kept in my trouser pocket, was missing.

Maddie started patting down my trousers, my jacket and turning out my handbag in a complete role reversal, while I stood trying not to panic, wracking my brains to remember if I'd left my phone in the apartment. I knew I'd taken a photo since then. Right behind the fear that someone might be able to access my bank account was the realisation that I'd lost all my contacts. Except the landlines I knew off by heart long before mobiles were invented, which amounted to Mum, my hairdresser and the doctor's surgery. But not Rico. I shouldn't even be having that thought. If ever there was a silver lining, it was that I hadn't had to delete his number but he was gone for good anyway. As he should be.

Maddie whipped out her phone. 'Right, we need to block your handset.'

'How do you do that?'

Suddenly, I really understood how my mother felt when she rang the doctor's and there was no option to speak to a human being, only a series of numbers to press that she couldn't hear anyway. I also got a guilty insight into how I made her feel when I said, 'Mum, it's easy. You just...'

Maddie was the picture of irritation, annoyed with me for delaying our sightseeing by being so careless in the first place, and compounded by my technological ineptitude. She was stabbing away at the screen. 'Find my Phone says it's around here somewhere.'

I looked around helplessly, as though I'd spot it lying at my feet. 'I think I was pickpocketed.'

'Mum, go outside and ask the blokes on the door if anything has been handed in.'

I wasn't sure when Maddie and I had swapped mother-daughter roles, but I meekly went off to ask the security guards, who barely disguised the 'yet another dumb tourist' eyeroll.

I walked back to Maddie, shaking my head.

She shrugged. 'It'll be fine. It's blocked. No one can get into it. And I've put my number on the front, so if anyone finds it, they can call me. I've set it up to play a sound to alert everyone that it's lost. Right, can we get on with the tour now?'

I would have liked to run up and down the streets looking for my phone, but I didn't want to spoil Maddie's day. I thanked her and we wandered through the rooms, with me telling her all the stories Rico had recounted. I pushed my worry about my mobile to one side and I allowed myself to luxuriate in observing how Maddie had grown up. Her ideas about the world were new, different from mine, independent. I felt both proud of who she was becoming and wistful for the days when she took my word as gospel.

Like me, she loved the Gallery of Maps. I deliberately averted my eyes from Sardinia, grateful when Maddie called my attention to the city names in Sicily being upside down. I narrowed my eyes, trying to remember what Rico had said. 'It's because the pope who commissioned this room wanted everything to look as it would if you were viewing it from Rome, and of course, Sicily is south from here.'

Despite the darts of sadness as I revisited the rooms, I loved Maddie's enthusiasm for the Sistine Chapel. 'Can we sit over here for a bit? That's my favourite part of the ceiling, where God is touching Adam's finger. I've got that poster in my bedroom at uni.'

I tried to relax into studying the art, but the security guards shouting at people for talking, taking photos and videos made me tense. As Maddie got her phone out to take a sneaky picture, I said, 'Don't do that.'

She tutted. 'You're such a rule follower, Mum,' but she put her mobile away.

I wished I could go through life doing whatever I pleased, not caring about what impression I gave or how other people might interpret my behaviour. But look how well that had turned out for me. One kiss with Rico while my husband was considering his options, which might or might not include other women, and I'd whipped up a right fiasco.

We spent the rest of the day walking miles, with Maddie openly impressed by how I knew my way around. I created a dot-to-dot of the best sights, slipping away from the crowds down alleyways and springing up again in a glorious square or viewpoint. We topped the afternoon off with a trip to my favourite ice cream parlour, Fata Morgana. I loved the glimpse of the child in my adult daughter as she studied the flavours, weighing up the pros and cons of the unusual – 'Pink grapefruit with ginger and horseradish, avocado with lime and white wine' – over her bog-standard favourites. I had developed a taste for coconut rum but instead chose the ones Maddie was fond of – cherry and vanilla – so we could swap if the liquorice and Kentucky chocolate with an infusion of tobacco leaves wasn't to her liking.

We went home for a rest before dinner and Maddie

vanished onto the terrace. She immersed herself in her phone, smiling and tapping away, lost in the company of other people I didn't even know. I didn't want to be clingy, so I said that I would FaceTime Helen from my laptop, explain about my phone so she could make work aware, in case they needed me for anything. As the call connected, I had the thought that Helen hadn't bothered with me much lately. It was surprising how quickly the grass grew over the hole you left behind. Work had sent panicky emails for the first month asking me what I'd done on various issues, but even that had tapered off.

However, she picked up straightaway. I told her what had happened. 'Honestly, the two girls weren't even as old as Maddie. I was stupid really, never occurred to me that's what they were up to. Anyway, thankfully Maddie was there so she blocked the phone. I'd have been right up a gumtree if I'd been on my own.'

'Maddie's there?'

'Yes, she surprised me yesterday.' I had a little burst of pride about being a mother who had a daughter who'd do that. 'Isn't it lovely to be young and carefree and hop on a plane on a whim? So great to see her, though.'

'Where is she now?' Helen asked.

'Out on the terrace soaking up every last bit of sun.'

I didn't want to admit that, like every other teenager, she was glued to her phone instead of reading up on the history of the Vatican, learning Italian and making the most of every single second in Rome.

Helen said, 'Right, I'm sorry, but I'd better go, Alan's calling me.'

Before we could say a proper goodbye, Maddie came in for a glass of water. I waved her over. 'Just say hi. I can't believe you two haven't ever met. Maddie, this is my friend Helen, you know, the one I work with, who helped me find this place.'

Out of screen shot, Maddie's face transitioned from the

reluctant 'Why are you introducing me to your boring friends?' to a bright smiley person who was a credit to me. She leaned into the screen.

Helen was saying, 'Sorry, I've really got to go.'

I couldn't see why she couldn't tell Alan to hold on a minute while she said a quick hello.

But in the seconds that she was stabbing at the off button, saying, 'I can never turn this thing off,' Maddie gasped.

The screen went blank. 'That's her, Mum.'

'What do you mean?'

'That's the woman who was having dinner with Dad at King's Cross, that evening, a couple of months ago.'

'Helen works with me, not with Dad, darling. Dad doesn't really know her.'

'Mum, it was definitely her. I'm certain it was, because I remember thinking that she was really young to be grey, but it kind of suited her. And she had that big locket thing on.'

Like some rusty farm machinery stored in a barn for fifty years and teased back to life by a very determined mechanic, the whole 'you've got that wrong' was giving way to the first tendrils of doubt. 'But I thought she was called Nicky?'

Maddie stared at me open-mouthed. 'What was Dad going to say? "Hello, love, this is your mother's friend, Helen whatever her surname is. Well, she used to be your mother's friend, but I'm shagging her now."'

A small part of my brain was scandalised that Maddie dared to use language like that in front of me. Yet again, I'd probably lost sight of the bigger picture.

'And you still believe they were having a sort of rendezvous?' I had no idea why I was resorting to language that made it sound like a romantic meeting of minds rather than calling a spade a spade and blurting out 'affair'. Affair. Affair. I couldn't fathom how Joel would even know Helen well enough to have dinner with her. 'Are you one hundred per cent sure it's her? This is serious, Maddie. Not something to be plucked out of the air because I do need to ask Dad about it.'

It would explain Helen getting so twitchy when I said Maddie was here. Maybe her waning interest in my time in Rome too, if the person she was actually most interested in was my husband. Like a blow to the stomach, I had a thought so horrible that I didn't even want to examine it. Helen 'Nicky' Nicholson had been instrumental in dispatching me to Rome in the first place. And stupid old me had been grateful, convinced that it was for my own good – 'You show him you're taking charge of your own life' – rather than a coast-clearing exercise.

Maddie held out her arms. 'I'm sorry, Mum.'

It turned out that it didn't matter whether you were in Purley or Rome, heartache had no borders.

16

When I woke up the next morning, I told myself that even if I damaged my facial muscles beyond repair, I was going to smile until Maddie had left for the airport that evening. I slipped out to buy one of nearly everything in the bakery and made a pot of coffee. By the time Maddie emerged bleary-eyed, my cocktail of fury and hurt was still swilling around a refusal to accept that what she'd said was true. One thing was clear to me, though: I wouldn't have another chance to hang out in Rome with my daughter in the near future and there was always plenty of time to be wretched. So sunny-side up, we were going to have a good day.

'Are you okay, Mum?'

'I'm fine, love. You don't need to worry about me or Dad. We'll sort things out. I'm not really sure what's going on there, but let's not spoil your stay over it.'

I was loving the confidence of the pretend me. I obviously did a brilliant acting job because her face went from anxious to interested in the dilemma between the pain au raisin or the almond croissant. There was a strong satisfaction in temporarily being able to absorb the worry of a child, even when that child was an adult. I was pretty sure my ability to wave a magic wand and fix things for Maddie was coming to an end, but I wasn't going to be defeated without one last sprinkle of fairy dust.

We ate ourselves to a standstill on a carb fest with no focaccia, croissant or mozzarella-topped pizza slice left unloved. 'Right, let's walk some of that off.'

Although the hopes for my marriage were burning like the stubble in autumn fields, I was bizarrely, doggedly, determined to enjoy every minute. No way was I going to allow whatever was waiting for me next to contaminate my happy moment with my woman-child daughter.

We hopped off the bus at Torre Argentina. Maddie was shaking her head. 'I can't get over how on every street, there are Roman ruins.'

'And these are ruins with a difference.' We leaned on the barriers surrounding the central square where columns and crumbling walls were overgrown with shrubs and grass. 'This is a cat sanctuary. Look. A bunch of feral cats took over the area and eventually a charity stepped in to look after them.' I pointed out all the moggies sunbathing on tumbledown plinths and the remains of the ancient temples. 'Julius Caesar was murdered here,' I said, my interesting historical fact nowhere near as fascinating to Maddie as the little ginger cat licking its paws on a chunk of Roman portico.

'Can we go in?'

I nodded. Maddie had always wanted a kitten, but Joel had been totally opposed to anything more demanding than a goldfish.

We went down the stairs into the underground office, where cats stalked about freely with a sense of ownership as though they were privy to the fact that they had taken up residence in one of the most desirable areas of Rome.

Maddie was particularly smitten with a tabby – Romolo –

with three legs and a purr like a chainsaw and a one-eyed fluff ball called Puffetta.

My mind kept drifting to Helen rushing off the FaceTime call and groping around for an explanation other than the obvious one. But I had to admit that a cat stretched out, demanding to have its stomach rubbed, was as good an antidote for heartbreak as any other I'd ever invented.

We spent three-quarters of an hour chatting to the volunteers and stroking the cats before coming away with half a gift shop's worth of calendars, pens and fridge magnets.

'That is so cool, I wish we could adopt Romolo,' Maddie said.

'Who knows? Maybe I'll move out to Rome permanently.'

Maddie went very still. 'Would you do that?'

'No, I don't think so. I wouldn't know where to start. I've loved my time here, though.' I couldn't help wishing I could postpone stepping onto the tarmac back home, when I'd no longer be able to dodge the next stage of life.

Maddie said, 'You'd work it out. Loads of people far thicker than you manage to move abroad.'

I laughed at her logic and her flimsy vote of confidence. 'Right, I'm taking you to my secret little corner of Rome now and you can pick your favourite painting.'

'Is it an art gallery?' she asked, failing to disguise the wrinkling of her nose.

'No. At least not in the sense you're thinking.'

I watched as her face struggled between adult holiday companion and teenage sulker who thought museums and galleries were 'full of old stuff'.

'Come on, it's ten minutes away, then it's ice cream time.'

I led her to Galleria Sciarra, which was a nineteenth-century covered walkway in the centre of an office building. After living in Rome, I was nervous of hyperbole, but I found the frescoes of female virtues breathtaking. Since Rico had shown me what he called 'the antidote to the madness of the Trevi Fountain', which was two minutes away, I'd returned several times. I spent ages staring up at the five storeys of paintings, all depicting women and paying homage to a range of supposedly desirable attributes including modesty, sobriety, mercy and faith.

'Wow. This is amazing. Imagine working in one of these offices,' Maddie said.

'I know. I keep asking myself if people who work in buildings like this still grump into work and lose their rag because the internet's gone down.'

We spent a while discussing which virtue we were going to pick. 'Well, I'm not having prudence,' Maddie said, putting the Latin inscriptions beneath the frescoes into Google Translate. 'And I'm definitely not having humility. She looks far too submissive.'

I loved her for that.

'I'm picking *fortis* – I'm assuming that's strength?'

'Good choice. That's very important in life.' Afraid of bringing down the mood, I cast my eyes about for a positive choice. 'I'll go with patience. We need a lot of that too.'

Maddie fired back, quick as a flash, 'Yeah, and look where that's got you.'

I tried not to feel blame in her words. To accept that how you viewed your parents' marriage – any marriage – at eighteen was nowhere near the attitude adjustment that was a privilege and a curse at fifty. But before I had a chance to absorb the stab of hurt that her words delivered, her mobile rang and the moment shrivelled away.

She frowned. 'Hello? What? Sorry I can't understand you.' She thrust the phone at me. 'It's some Italian woman.'

Between my limited Italian and the caller's few words of English, I understood that she had found my phone and that she was with her family on the steps outside the Vatican museums.

'Can you wait for me, fifteen minutes, please?'

She agreed and Maddie and I jumped in a cab. It only occurred to me as we got out that I had no idea what she looked like.

Maddie was much more logical than I was. 'She said she was with her family. So maybe a mum and dad with kids?'

I stayed focused on locating the woman, rather than getting sucked into how Maddie's and my image of 'family' might have to change.

We ran down the steps, where I spotted a girl about Maddie's age, standing with an older couple I assumed were her parents. She was holding my turquoise phone. I practically threw myself on her with gratitude, and offered her twenty euro, which they all batted away. She managed to communicate that they were also on holiday and had spotted it discarded under a parked car. But, most of all, they were sorry that I would have such a horrible memory of Rome. After a lot of miming and me telling them that Rome had my heart, we finished our conversation with a big hug all round.

'How often does that happen, Maddie, that you get pick-pocketed and actually recover your stuff?' I felt quite giddy with the goodness and generosity of some people, thrilled to have proof that there were gorgeous humans in the world, as well as – if Maddie was correct – ones like Helen. The screen showed a host of text messages from Joel. 'Dad wants me to ring him,' I said, irritated that he was encroaching on my last precious hours with Maddie.

'I bet he bloody does.'

'You haven't said anything to him about Helen, have you?'

'Of course I have! I WhatsApp'd him last night, but he hasn't answered me. I don't understand why you didn't ring him the minute I saw her on FaceTime. You're letting him get away with everything.'

And with that, she burst into tears, stomping off past the

crowds milling about waiting to enter the museum. A few people swivelled round as she shouted but soon drifted back to their own uncomplicated lives.

I hurried after her, cursing the heat of the afternoon as my hair stuck to my neck. I caught up with her. 'Maddie, I wasn't letting it go. I just wanted to make the most of being with you today. I was going to call him tonight after I'd seen you off to the airport.'

I felt helpless and longed to turn the clock back to when I could fix everything. When the keys to Maddie's happiness – another go on the swings, chocolate for pudding, a second bedtime story – weren't outside my control. In the middle of the throng of people, I held her while she cried, my heart still refusing to believe that Joel could be having an affair with Helen. Maddie had so much more courage than me. She really was the definition of *fortis*. I, on the other hand, was beginning to think that instead of patience, I should have chosen good old humility, sitting there submissively in her apron, as my defining virtue.

17

That evening, after I'd waved Maddie off to the airport, I slumped onto a bench on the railway platform. I finally released every emotion I'd been smothering and sobbed until I was exhausted. Which wasn't the best frame of mind for calling Joel, but it suddenly struck me that he wasn't sitting in a shattered heap in a foreign station, feeling as though he'd failed in every way. My plan to make a calm list of what I definitely knew and what I needed to ask flew out the window. I turned my back on the trains chugging in and out and rang him.

I'd expected him to try to convince me that Maddie was totally mistaken, that it wasn't Helen at all, but as soon as he picked up, he said, 'Bethie, I'm so sorry. Neither of us meant for anything to happen.'

I'd been braced for forcing the truth out of him and the straightforward confirmation winded me. Until then, I'd deluded myself that there was a simple explanation that would make everything right.

Joel's admission lit a flame of rage that freed my thoughts and resentments from the cage that they'd been pawing at, waiting to break out. 'So why visit a few weeks ago? Double-checking you were making the right decision?' I felt sick to my stomach that I'd slept with the man who'd been having sex with my friend. Like a coin dropping into an empty charity tin, realisation reverberated around my brain. 'She told you. She told you that someone was interested in me. And, like a total bastard, you came out to pee on your territory, to pretend that there was still hope for us, instead of being honest and releasing me.'

Joel ignored my questions to ask some of his own. 'Just put me out of my misery. Was it that guy singing? Where the view was? He kept staring after you.'

I walked out of the station, away from the noise of the trains rumbling about. I found myself pushing past other tourists, my pace fast and furious as I steeled myself for Joel's scorn if I told him the truth, for his cruel, dismissive opinion of a street busker. I couldn't hear it. Couldn't bear his sarcastic mirth about me going from someone who worked in financial institutions to someone who collected coins in a guitar case.

'You don't get to ask any questions. You need to answer mine.'

'But was he the one?'

I ignored him. 'So are you planning to set up house together? What does Alan think about it? Presumably he's aware that the whole "looking after the elderly parents" is a euphemism for weekends away with you?' I remembered ringing Helen's phone and the tone sounding different, elongated, as though she was abroad. She'd convinced me it was because she was in the Isle of Wight at her parents', rather than having a lovers' tryst in Paris in some romantic mansard. How they must have laughed at my stupidity, my gullibility.

'He doesn't know. Please don't tell him. Helen and I, we're not a thing. It was a mistake. It's over. I finished it not long after I left you in Rome.'

I'd really have preferred to hear that he'd rushed home to fix things as best he could *that very evening*.

'How did you even get to know her?'

'We met at that Christmas party. It was during that awful period when I was working in annuity insurance. She emailed me, wanting a bit of informal advice about the best way to fund a care home for her mother. I met her for a coffee.'

'That was two years ago! You never mentioned it.' All I could remember about that time was how miserable Joel had been and how it had been a relief when he'd handed in his notice even though he'd been unemployed for a few months afterwards.

'It didn't seem very ethical to discuss her financial affairs with you.'

The brass neck of the man took my breath away. 'I'd absolutely love to understand where your ethics fitted in to sleeping with your wife's friend, you upstanding pillar of the community, you.'

'I know how it sounds. You won't believe how sorry I am. I think I was suffering from the whole cliché of a midlife crisis, the sudden realisation that so many years are behind us. But please, come home. You're hurt now, of course you are, but I still don't want to throw away our marriage. I love you, I really do. I've been a total idiot.' His voice trembled. 'Please, Beth. Don't tell me that twenty-four years count for nothing.' I'd never heard so much emotion from Joel in one day, let alone in half an hour. I was finally hearing the words I'd been waiting for but there was no rush of triumph.

'It's a lot to take in. How would I even go about forgiving you?'

'Think of Maddie. How happy she'd be if we sorted things out and we could be the family we were before. We wouldn't have to sell the house; Maddie would have a proper base instead of shuttling between the two of us.'

'Perhaps you should have thought about Maddie before you started the whole shenanigans with Helen.'

But Joel did make rowing back to the status quo sound appealing. Even so, it was depressing that my knee-jerk reaction was to lean towards reacquainting myself with the devil I knew, rather than diving into a terrifying sea of change. Weariness engulfed me.

'I'll be home next week. I'll tell you then.'

I'd keep Joel waiting for a whole six days after he'd kept me dangling for nearly eight months. Never let it be said that I was a woman who didn't know how to exact revenge. Maybe I could do a better job on Helen. I'd need to get some sleep first.

18

The next day I was not so much called as summoned to Ronnie's apartment. There was a certain gravitas about her manner, that quiet air of a woman who'd seen a lot, knew a lot, but only voiced a fraction of her thoughts. The opposite of Marina, whose words poured out like water through a colander.

Ronnie waved me in. 'You've had a busy time of it. I loved your daughter. She's got her head screwed on. She'll go far.'

I waited for Ronnie to provide me with evidence, preferably something that I could trace to my own glittering parenting, because right now, I needed all the bolstering I could get.

Instead, she asked, 'So are you looking forward to going back to Blighty?'

I meant to thank her for this opportunity, for offering a total stranger a place to reset and reconsider. I wanted to tell her that I wasn't expecting her to host me, but that I was intending to return for another couple of months in the future. She could absolutely consider her experiment a success.

As I opened my mouth to say those things, a sob swelled up in a splutteringly non-British way. Within minutes, I was installed on her turquoise sofa, hiccupping out the whole story,

too distressed to put any spin on it to save my dignity or protect
Joel from her disdain. If indeed we did somehow manage to cut
up an eiderdown the size of the universe and patchwork over
our marital debacle, we'd have to contend with her disapproval.
Strega clambered onto my lap and licked my hand. With every
sentence I uttered, I realised the truth that I'd refused to admit
to myself. Joel and I were history. That ship had sailed. And
somewhere in a deep recess, buried beneath the hurt and the
wishing that it were different, the first twinkle of relief flashed
through me that I didn't have to mould myself to what he
wanted. I could simply be me. Alone. Divorced. But myself.
Another day, if not today, that would count for something.

Ronnie made me tea, warming the pot first, which even in
my upset I noted was a peculiarly old-fashioned British habit
that hadn't faded in the forty-five years she'd been in Italy. In a
week of so much change, it was oddly comforting. She stirred
the pot, her eyes darting about, her head nodding imperceptibly
as if she were arguing with someone in her head.

Within minutes, Marina appeared, ever-present at the first
sign of drama. I resigned myself to receiving her acerbic advice,
which, although not tactfully presented, often contained
wisdom beneath the barbs. Ronnie filled her in.

'And what does the "friend" say?' she asked.

'I haven't spoken to her. I sent her a voice message, quietly
pointing out that her behaviour was despicable and that I found
her very disappointing as a human being.' I didn't add that I'd
blocked her number so that she had no right of reply.

Marina slapped the table. 'Why didn't you ring her? At least
blow the whistle on her with her husband?'

'I'm not certain what I'd gain from it. There isn't a single
excuse she can come up with that will make me feel better.
Knowing Helen, she's more likely to attack me than apologise
and that's going to make me angrier. And frankly, being stuck
with Alan for the rest of her life is punishment enough.'

Ronnie nodded. 'I think you're probably very wise.'

Marina threw her hands up. 'I don't understand you English. You're going to let her have an affair with your husband, the conniving little witch who encouraged you out here in the first place so she could play mousey mousey while the cat was away – and not take a moment to put her on the spot?'

If I hadn't felt as though my heart had all the resilience of sand in a sieve, I could have laughed at Marina's shock that I might sidestep a showdown. 'Perhaps you'd like to speak to her in my place.'

She adjusted her pearls. 'What's her number? I'd like to give her a piece of my razor-sharp mind.'

Ronnie batted her away. 'Marina! The best revenge is to be happy.'

Marina didn't miss a beat. 'Well, that and making everyone who has wronged you suffer.'

Ronnie sighed. 'Not everyone is like you. Beth is far more forgiving.'

'Tell me you're never going to forgive that husband. I didn't like him. Didn't have a shred of shame about his behaviour.'

Ronnie tried to shut her up. 'You only spoke to him for five minutes. No one has any idea about what goes on in other people's marriages.'

The upside of this conversation was that there was nothing Marina could say that would make me feel more stupid than I already did.

Marina rubbed her fingers over the teeth of the silver skull that topped her walking stick. 'Maybe not, but if he's having sex with her friend, you can be sure that none of it's good. You'll have to do one last challenge and we'll see if we can knock some sense into you.'

Ronnie frowned. 'We haven't discussed this.'

Marina smirked. 'I've had a brilliant idea.'

I was pretty sure that there was an entire gulf between Marina's brilliant and my half-palatable. And she could go off and condescend somewhere else. My best guest do-as-I-was-told compliance had evaporated. 'I'm not doing any more challenges.'

Life was testing enough. I didn't want to shop for fresh basil, find a fountain with a turtle on it or prance about in vintage clothes to prove I was young at heart. I simply hankered after an uncomplicated existence, with a man who loved me and a daughter who was settled and secure. It might seem mind-numbing to Marina, and maybe Ronnie too, but this clinging onto a rollercoaster in search of adventure wasn't all it was cracked up to be either.

They both ignored me.

Marina got up and beckoned Ronnie into the hallway. Whispered Italian and a few exclamations ensued before they returned with Ronnie saying, 'I don't know how I've stayed friends with you for so long.'

Rebellion bubbled within me. 'Whatever it is, I'm not interested.'

'You'll love this challenge,' Ronnie said. 'In fact, don't even think of it like that. It's simply an outing to a place you shouldn't miss. You know where the area called Testaccio is, near the keyhole of the Knights of Malta? There's a non-Catholic ceme-tery over that way. Keats and Shelley are buried there. It has a fabulous view over the Pyramid of Cestius, which you shouldn't leave Rome without seeing.'

'What do I have to do when I get there?' I said, sulky as a teenager wary of being tricked into visiting an ageing aunt.

Marina chimed in. 'Nothing. Just look around and ask your-self if you died tomorrow, or let's be generous, in the next two years, have you lived your best life?'

'That's a cheery challenge.'

Marina laughed. 'Every time I go there, I come home and

drink a bottle of Amarone on the grounds that if I'm going to feed the worms sooner rather than later, I want to make sure I've drunk all my best wine.'

I didn't have the energy to argue, and actually, I'd always found cemeteries quite fascinating. 'I'll go this afternoon.'

Marina winked at Ronnie. 'See. Who can resist a trip to a graveyard?'

With uncharacteristic wit, Ronnie said, 'You'll be the death of me.'

They both fell about like two slapstick characters from the silent movies. Annoying as they were, I'd miss them.

I'd decided I was too lazy to walk all that way, but in the end, I let the bus rattle on past me. Walking had become an addiction. My whole body felt better when I was on the move, noticing the tiny intricate details of the city I'd come to love. Even in my broken state, I still found it in me to admire the ornate drinking fountains dotted on the streets, the rowers gliding down the Tiber, the elegance of an old lady sitting in her fur coat on this sunny May afternoon. Admittedly, there was the whisper of a breeze, but nothing significant enough to have stopped London's working population pouring out into the parks in their lunch break. In fact, I was so spoilt with all the spring sunshine, this would probably count as high summer at home.

I strolled through Testaccio, admiring the juxtaposition of ancient walls and the blossom and foliage that took up residence on them, disrespectful of their age. I even loved the graffiti art opposite the cemetery, the doleful faces with the knowing eyes of old men to whom very little would come as a shock. The women sitting at the entrance to the graveyard offered me a leaflet. I accepted out of politeness but wandered off in a random direction without consulting it.

Despite my annoyance at Marina, the shady peace among

the trees stilled the churning of my mind, the stomach-flipping cycle of forgetting, then remembering, interrupted. There was something soothing about the old stones, the sense of the cycle of life. The myriad ways that people tried to show their loved ones that they were still important with flowers, pictures and presents made my heartbreak seem a little less all-consuming. It was the first place I'd been in Rome that was practically deserted.

I stumbled across Shelley's grave, pondering the words inscribed there: 'Nothing of him that doth fade/But doth suffer a sea-change/Into something rich and strange'. On my phone, I searched for the poet's connection to this site, shaking my head as I saw that Shelley's three-year-old son was also buried here. As I sat reading about Shelley's death in a shipwreck, I agreed wholeheartedly with what he had written to his friend in 1818 – 'The English burying-place is a green slope near the walls, under the pyramidal tomb of Cestius, and, as I think, the most beautiful and solemn cemetery I have ever beheld.'

I spent ages listening to the birdsong, the underlying hum of traffic, wondering whether my own sea change could turn into something rich and preferably not too strange. Then I stood up, furious with myself for looking for meaning in everything, when probably the real meaning was that Joel didn't love me any more and I'd been too afraid to face up to that. Never mind rich and strange, anything better than completely cynical about men forever more would be a bonus.

I passed the Angel of Grief, a sculpture of a weeping angel collapsed in despair on a tomb. According to the leaflet, it was a memorial to an American sculptor's wife, who described her as 'My stay, my joy, my help in all things.' I couldn't linger. This wasn't a day when I needed reminders that some men adored their wives forever and never wanted anything else. Lucky you, Emelyn Story. I hurried away, astonished that I could be envious of a woman who died in 1894.

I looked at the map to see where the Pyramid of Cestius was situated and wandered over to the far corner. As I leaned on the railing, I wished Maddie was with me to see yet more cats lounging about sunning themselves in the splendid surroundings of an ancient tomb built for a wealthy magistrate.

A shadow fell over me and I jolted round.

Rico. I gasped, feeling as though all the oxygen, blood, whatever it was that kept bodies upright and hearts beating in a steady rhythm, was leaving my body.

He had his guitar slung over his shoulder. His face wasn't smiling, but his eyes were. The great rush of delight at seeing him immediately reminded me of what I'd said to Maddie to encourage her to sift through her complex emotions. *'You can't help the way you feel. What you can help is how you manage those feelings.'*

I was obviously going to be a victim of my own smart-alec advice, because I didn't want to manage my feelings at all. I wanted to let them gallop loose, with me butt-naked and hanging onto their mane. I wrestled that initial surge of emotion into a far less off-putting 'Hello! Have you come to sing here?' though when I reflected on this afterwards, the amount of people in the cemetery who still had the ability to chuck in five-euro notes wouldn't have made it the most sensible choice of venue.

He shook his head. 'I came to see you.'

I did a nervous laugh. 'First the crypt and now a graveyard. We know how to live life.'

Rico pulled a face. 'I'm not sure we do.'

There was a silence.

A sturdy tom cat came purring around Rico's bare legs, miaowing for attention. He squatted down to stroke it. 'Hey, you. You're friendly.'

The cat's spine rippled under his hand as those long fingers pressed gently into his fur.

He stood up. 'I want to show you a grave. It's my favourite.'

I loved that he had a favourite grave. I'd also identified the one that had really moved me – a young man, barely older than Maddie, with a dog and a book. If I'd remarked on that to Joel, he would have told me to get a grip and said, 'You're such a weirdo'.

Rico led me through the shade of the trees to a small square grave topped with a case that said 'Musik', a skipping rope, a ball and a little wicker basket. Gerda Salzmann. 2 October 1897 to 2 January 1908.

'Why do you like this one the best? She was only ten. It's so sad.'

'Because it gives a sense of who she was. I imagine her as a sporty girl who loved nature, being outside, but also thoughtful. I prefer to think if she'd lived, she would have become a wonderful violinist. I come here every time, to let her know she hasn't been forgotten,' Rico said. 'But most of all, the words make me feel here.' He patted his hand over his heart.

I stared at the German words around the base of the headstone. '*Das Wort ABSCHIED ist ein gar trauriges Wort.*' I wished I was an international polyglot who could nod and make an incisive comment to show I had no need of Google Translate.

'You'll have to help me with that.'

He took a step towards me. 'The word "farewell" is such a sad word.'

In the last few months, the surreal moments outnumbered all those of the preceding years put together. Me in a cemetery welling up over a little girl I never knew who died over a hundred years ago. Not to mention the close proximity of a guy who was quite wrong for me but somehow had a hold over my heart that my brain couldn't overrule.

Rico leaned his guitar against a neighbouring headstone. 'I don't want to say farewell to you.'

Of course it would have been far too easy for me to say, 'Ditto. So given that we both feel the same, that's not a problem.'

Instead I said, 'I'm going home on Wednesday anyway,' in the manner of someone who was weighing up what would be most cost-effective, given the time limit: a weekly bus ticket or single journeys.

Rico pushed his fringe out of his eyes. 'So that's it? You leave Rome forever?'

My throat tightened against a swell of sadness as I said, 'I'll come back to see Ronnie, probably, at some point. And Marina.' Suddenly, the penny dropped. 'Marina rang you, didn't she?'

Rico nodded. 'She doesn't like the idea of you running back to your husband.'

'It's actually none of her business,' I said, not quite achieving the height of outrage I was aiming for. 'But she's got her wish. My marriage is over.' As I said the words out loud, something in me steadied, the conviction of making a hard decision but categorically the right one.

Rico put his hand on my arm. 'Once I knew you were here and what had happened with your friend and Joel...' He cleared his throat as though simply articulating his name required a subsequent dislodging action. 'I had to see you. If only for the farewell.' He pulled his sunglasses off the top of his head and put them on. 'Tell me right now that you don't feel anything for me and I will walk away. But before you do that, look around you. Everyone, everyone here in this *cimitero*, would have snatched at a second chance, an opportunity to love a bit more, for longer, to feel good things, to have more experiences. To have their heart beat for the purpose of love, not only to send blood round their body so they can, I don't know, have enough air in their lungs to walk to the shops.'

And somehow, what I meant to say, that I couldn't get involved with anyone until I'd seen Joel face-to-face, dissipated into the atmosphere. Unlike Rico's words, the ones that I did utter weren't going to win the romantic speech of the century: 'I can't kiss you here, it's a graveyard. It's not very respectful.'

Rico let out a huge sigh. 'If I was dead, I would be ecstatic that people were kissing by my tomb. Maybe I will have that as my epitaph. *Bacia pure*. Feel free to kiss.' He leaned towards me. 'Be a rebel for once in your life. Please.'

In that moment, that day in May, I decided I would practise breaking a few rules. For everyone who could no longer kiss their loved ones, that one was for you.

A LETTER FROM KERRY

Dear Reader,

I want to say a huge thank you for choosing to read *The Rome Apartment*. If you did enjoy it, and want to keep up to date with all my latest releases, just sign up at the following link. Your email address will never be shared and you can unsubscribe at any time.

www.bookouture.com/kerry-fisher

I lived in Florence and Tuscany for five years in my twenties, working as a grape picker, a holiday rep, a guidebook researcher and a personal assistant to the director of an art school. Most of the ex-pat friends I made while I was living there have eventually found their way back to their home countries, but we have remained united, thirty years on, by our love for Italy (and each other!). We all agree that there is something magical about that country and all of us over the years have returned regularly.

In 2022, my husband and I finally had the opportunity to spend a month in Rome. I hadn't planned for our time there to be a research trip, viewing it instead as a chance to live in the city and experience it in a different way from my usual approach to sightseeing (which is to get up at the crack of dawn and race about trying to see everything in four days!). I had dipped a toe in the water writing scenes against an Italian backdrop before – the country has a cameo role in *After the Lie, The Silent Wife* and *The Woman I Was Before* – but I've never set an entire book there.

However, as soon as I arrived in Rome, the creative possibilities started jostling for attention – it's hard to ignore the inspiration offered up by all those eye-catching doorways and the enticing courtyards beyond, the little curiosities around every corner.

It was an absolute privilege to experience a month away from 'normal life' – the luxury of time to dream, to wander and wonder without the daily urgency to get things done. Rome has an energy all of its own – I walked miles and miles every day and could have stayed for much longer without tiring of it. No matter how often I passed through the same streets, there was always something new to see – the gesticulating inherent in any conversation, a stained-glass window catching the sun, olive oil sold from the bonnet of a car, the Swiss Guards emerging in their colourful uniforms from an alleyway, an impromptu dance display near the Colosseum, the stylish hats and gloves...

My husband did get pickpocketed at the Vatican and a wonderful Italian family did find his phone and return it to us. I was delighted by the proof that there are more good people in the world than bad!

I found my whole time there so invigorating. Consequently, it wasn't a huge leap to come up with a scenario about how a woman at a crossroads in her life might benefit from a spell in a city that radiates vitality and joy to help her change her perspective on life. *The Rome Apartment* was the result and I hope you loved it. If you did, I would be very grateful if you could write a review. I'd love to know what you think, and it makes a real difference in helping new readers to discover one of my books for the first time.

I love hearing from my readers – you can get in touch on my Facebook page, through Twitter, or my website. Whenever I hear from readers, I am reminded why I love my job – your messages never fail to brighten my day.

Thank you so much for reading,

Kerry Fisher

www.kerryfisherauthor.com

 facebook.com/kerryfisherauthor
twitter.com/KerryFSwayne

ACKNOWLEDGEMENTS

'Thank you' seems a rather underwhelming expression for the gratitude I feel for the support of my editor, Jenny Geras. Her vision always plays a significant role in transforming my scrappy, half-baked ideas into fully-formed stories – a feat she pulls off with grace and patience.

Huge thanks to the Bookouture production team working their magic to make the finished product the best it can possibly be – plus the wonderful publicity team – Kim, Noelle, Sarah and Jess – who do a great job of connecting our books with the right readership.

Thank you to the brilliant Clare Wallace, my agent at Darley Anderson – I've been so lucky to have you championing my books over the last ten years.

I couldn't finish my acknowledgements without saying a massive thank you to all my readers – you are the best cheer-leaders – I love the conversations and interactions I have with you on my author Facebook page. Your enthusiasm for my books really gives me a lift when the going gets tough. For this book, in particular, I appreciated all your suggestions for the song that Beth might hear to give her hope the first time she sees Rico at the Giardino degli Aranci. I chose 'Here Comes the Sun', suggested by Jo Leah, but had a wonderful time wearing out Alexa listening to all your ideas!

Thank you also to the lovely Mira, who made us so welcome at her apartment near the Vatican – we couldn't have loved our stay there more.

Finally, to my husband, Steve, for sharing the Italian adventure with me and waiting patiently in cafés while I indulged my passion for foreign cemeteries.

Made in the USA
Las Vegas, NV
05 October 2023

78553028R00121